DOCTOR DAVID

Carla works in her father's bookshop, but when her fiancé Emile leaves her for her sister Jane, she decides to get away before the wedding.

She heads for Ravensford in Yorkshire, where her family used to spend holidays, and turns up at the hotel where they used to stay, to find a peculiar welcome: a man ushers her hastily into the kitchen, telling her she is late, before dashing off himself! The hotel has now, she discovers, become a hostel for retired show people. The woman who runs it is ill in hospital and her son, Dr David Ross, who greeted Carla so unexpectedly, offers her the job of cook in the wake of their little misunderstanding.

Carla is fascinated by the doctor while she works there, but is despondent on learning he has a wife in America. Yet if this is so why should he seem to resent her friendship with her neighbour Robin so much, and how can there possibly be any happy outcome of her rapidly growing love . . . ?

DOCTOR DAVID

RAINBOW ROMANCE

by

Margaret Allan

ROBERT HALE · LONDON

© Margaret Allan 1989
First published in Great Britain 1989

ISBN 0 7090 3590 X

Robert Hale Limited
Clerkenwell House
Clerkenwell Green
London EC1R 0HT

To Julia and Mike

Photoset by PRG Graphics
Printed in Great Britain by St Edmundsbury Press Ltd,
Bury St Edmunds, Suffolk.
Bound by Hunter and Foulis Ltd.

One

'It's for you, Carla.' Her father smiled at her as he moved towards the door that led into the book-shop, leaving her to take the telephone call in private.

A rush of joy invaded Carla as she spoke to the man on the other end of the line, a pulsating excitement that pushed away the smell of old books and an old building, and evoked instead the scent of Emile's spicy aftershave lotion and his slim, expensive cigars.

'Emile,' she said softly, hesitantly, because even now she could hardly think of him without feeling a sense of wonder that he should fall in love with her.

'How are you, my sweet?' He did not wait to hear how she was, but went on at once, 'I ring to give my apologies, and to ask for your understanding because I can't manage to see you tonight after all.'

Crushing disappointment flooded her being as she waited for him to explain. She listened while he went on, in his charmingly accented voice, to tell her of the big function to be held tonight in the restaurant owned by his parents and managed by him. Yet surely he must have known about that function when he asked her to go out with him, a small voice inside her whispered.

'I hope you will not be too disappointed. It is something that cannot be helped, and you know how I hate to let you down like this — '

'Of course.' Carla swallowed. It was the second time that week he had cancelled a date with her, but she would not let him know how hurt she felt. 'I know how important the restaurant is to you.'

'It is my whole future. One day it will be mine.' A few murmured words of Italian to someone who must have interrupted the call gave Carla time to reflect that not so long ago Emile had told her that she was his future, the most important thing in his life. She shivered, and waited for him to give all his attention to her again. To arrange another meeting.

'I must ring off, there is a crisis. Something I must attend to. I'll be in touch later, my sweet,' was all he had to say to her before the call ended.

Frowning, she went through into the bookshop, where her father was just seeing out the last customer of the day and bidding the man who had bought only a cheap paperback the same courteous 'Goodnight, Sir' as he would have extended to one of the academics who spent large sums with the family business: Locking the front door, and turning the sign round so that it read CLOSED, he gave Carla a teasing smile.

'Couldn't Emile wait another hour or so to talk to you? He must be keen,' he joked as he began to empty the cash register.

'He was ringing to cancel our date. He can't

make it tonight because there's a big function at the restaurant and he needs to be there.'

'Rather short notice, wasn't it? I mean, he must have had some idea, if it's such an important affair. It won't have all happened at the last minute.' Her father was frowning now.

'I think some sort of crisis came up.' Carla kept her voice carefully casual but the same thought had already occurred to her. She wondered why Emile had not asked her to go along and help with this big party, as she had already done a few times. He must have known that she would enjoy helping, rather than being left at a loose end for the evening.

'Since you are free after all, why not come to the theatre with us?' her father suggested.

'You won't be able to get a seat for me now,' Carla began, but the phone rang again so she hurried to answer it.

The caller was her sister. Jane, the prettier, older Bradley girl who had returned to the family home a few weeks ago after spending some months in Canada.

'I wanted to speak to Dad, but you'll do Carla. It's just that I can't get back in time to go to the theatre tonight with Dad and Helen,' she explained.

'Will you meet them there?'

'No. I won't be going at all. I can't make it.'

'Are you working late?'

A moment of hesitation, long enough for Carla to wonder if it was the truth, then, 'Yes.'

'But I thought — '

'Must ring off. Someone else wants the phone.'

That was Jane, Carla thought wryly, always in a hurry. Always changing her mind too, about things, people, work, plans. Jane had gone to Canada to prepare a home ready for her marriage to the Canadian lawyer she had become engaged to after a whirlwind romance, then changed her mind about him and come home.

'It was Jane. She can't make it tonight, Dad,' she told him, back in the shop.

'Did she say why?'

'She's working late, she said.'

'Is she? I wonder − ' He looked displeased.

'You'll be able to come with us after all then, Carla,' Helen Ford, the middle-aged widow who had taken Jane's place in the family business, remarked. 'I'm sure you'll enjoy the play. It's had some very good reviews.'

'We're eating at a little place near the theatre. Why don't you go upstairs and get ready while I take the cash over to the night safe?' her father added.

Carla tried to push away her disappointment as she changed out of her plain blouse and skirt into the pretty, patterned silk matching skirt and shirt she had been planning to wear for her evening with Emile. The feeling of having been let down by Emile persisted, even when she was enjoying a delicious early supper in the company of her father and Helen. It stayed with her throughout the play, in spite of the fact that this was well acted and moving. She was aware all the time of a sense of foreboding, a feeling that things were about to go wrong for her, even though she told herself that it was stupid to get so upset just because Emile had put his business before her for the second time that week.

After the play they took Helen back to her suburban flat and stayed to have coffee with her, but while her father and Helen talked cheerfully Carla was for the most part silent and withdrawn. She was glad when it was time for them to drive back to the flat above the bookshop.

'You're very quiet tonight, Carla,' her father commented as they drove homewards through the still busy streets of London.

'I'm tired,' she hedged.

'And disappointed?'

'No, I've enjoyed the evening,' she lied.

'But not as much as you'd have enjoyed being with Emile.' He gave her a long, perceptive look as they waited at traffic lights. 'Don't care *too* much my dear. Don't let yourself be hurt.'

'I won't,' she said quickly.

Yet the hurt was not to be avoided. It was there waiting for her in the flat above the bookshop where she saw, as soon as she opened the door into the sitting-room, that Emile and Jane were sitting close together on the big sofa.

'Emile!' Her eyes widened with astonishment. 'I didn't expect to see you.'

She felt, in that moment, a tremor of fear. Then her father put an arm about her shoulders, holding her firmly.

'Jane said we should come and tell you at once.' Emile stopped speaking, plainly ill at ease, then continued with a rush. 'She said we must not go on meeting as we have been doing, in secret.'

Carla felt her heart lurch. 'In secret,' she heard

herself whisper. 'Why should you do that?' Yet even as she asked the question she could guess at the answer to it.

'We are in love, you see, Jane and me.' Emile said the words with a touch of defiance. 'It was something neither of us could help. It just happened.'

Carla tore her stricken gaze away from his face and waited for her sister to speak. She did not have long to wait.

'We want to get married fairly soon. I'm going to move into the flat above the restaurant with Emile then. The flat is almost ready, so I won't need to wait.'

That was typical of Jane, direct as always, and, in a hurry, as always. Too much of a hurry to be aware of the hurt she was causing. Or didn't she care about that? Carla wondered.

Alex Bradley was angry with his older daughter. 'It isn't so long since you were planning to marry Howard and live in Canada,' he reminded her. 'Are you certain you know your own mind this time, Jane?'

Jane smiled at him, her lovely face glowing with happiness. 'Oh yes, Dad, I'm quite certain, and so is Emile.'

There was a great lump swelling inside Carla's throat. How could Emile be so certain when only a short time ago he had said he loved *her*, and shown *her* over the flat which was being renovated? That was the day before Jane arrived back from Canada, she recalled. She swallowed, and tried hard to think of something to say. But there was nothing she could say, not without breaking down and making a fool of herself before them all. She was glad, so glad, to feel her father's arm strong about her shoulders, supporting her, willing her to keep calm.

It was her father who spoke next to Jane. 'There's nothing I can do to stop you, since you are old enough to please yourself about these things, but I find it too soon, and too sudden, to be able to give you my wholehearted approval. In fact, my advice to you both would be to wait a while before marrying. Though I know you are unlikely to take notice of what I think, even for your sister's sake,' he could not resist adding.

'Why should we? It's not as if Emile had been serious about Carla, is it?' As always, Jane tried to justify her actions.

Emile looked distinctly uncomfortable now. Alex Bradley looked angry. Jane went on smiling and holding Emile's hand. Carla knew that she could not stand much more, that she had to escape. She took a deep breath, and found words at last.

'As you say, and as Emile seems to agree, it was nothing serious with us. We were just going around together when he had nothing else to do with his time — ' Her voice gave way then and she tore herself free of her father's comforting arm to stumble out of the room, along the landing and up the next flight of stairs to her bedroom.

For a long time she lay on her bed willing herself not to cry, telling herself that it really did not matter that Emile was going to marry Jane and not her, knowing all the time that it mattered terribly because since Emile had come into her life he had become the centre of it. She had been deeply depressed after the premature death of her mother, and he had cheered her enormously with his ebullient personality, his charm and his good looks.

During the next few days she felt numb and unable to find her usual enjoyment and interest in her work in the bookshop. When she was in the flat above, sharing meals with her father and Jane, she felt raw with hurt as Jane talked too often of Emile and their wedding plans. She began to dread those mealtimes, to dread having to be in the company of her sister when she was so intensely jealous of her happiness. Almost, she began to hate her sister.

It all came to a head early one morning when the two girls and their father were sharing breakfast before the bookshop opened for business. Carla had endured yet another sleepless night and knew that she looked drab and weary so that the sight of her sister's radiant face brought a fresh stab of pain to her. Then Jane began to talk about the wedding dresses she had been looking at.

'If I have the ivory velvet, you could wear apricot velvet Carla,' she said in between spooning grapefruit into her mouth. 'It would look gorgeous for an early December wedding.'

Carla dropped her grapefruit spoon with a clatter and sprang to her feet, a torrent of words spilling out of her. 'For heaven's sake shut up! I'm sick of hearing you go on about the wedding! I don't care what you wear, and as for what you want me to wear you can save your breath because I won't be there. So there's no point in discussing it.'

'Of course, you'll be there! You'll be my bridesmaid. I've got it all planned — '

How could Jane be so insensitive, Alex Bradley wondered as he watched his daughters with growing dismay. This had gone deep with Carla. Too deep, and he was frightened for her.

'Well you can just unplan it,' Carla declared. 'Because I'm not interested.'

Before either of them could stop her she was out of the room and out of the flat, hurrying along the pavement as fast as she could go, jostling the office-workers and the shopgirls who were now emerging from buses and the tube station. The early morning breeze was cold on her thinly clad shoulders but she did not notice it as she stumbled on and on, not knowing where she was heading for. Not caring either. She was unaware of the curious glances directed at her by some of the passers-by. All she could see in her mind was Jane, radiant and beautiful in a long white velvet gown, walking hand in hand with Emile.

Suddenly then she found herself confronted by a whole window full of wedding gowns as she was elbowed aside by a hurrying youth. There were other things too, things like silver sandals and posies of pastel coloured flowers, but Carla saw only the white dresses and all her own shattered dreams. She turned her back on the window and began to run, this time across the road and into the park.

On the broad walks there were less people to impede her, but more people to look at her with concern because now it was raining and she wore no coat. Carla ignored them and ran on until she came to a summer house, where she shut herself in with her misery. For a long time she stood there watching the rain pouring down from a steel grey sky, too unhappy to care that she ought long since to have been helping her father and Helen in the bookshop.

Of one thing only was she certain, that she could not go on living at home and listening daily to Jane talking about her wedding to Emile. She would go out of her mind if she had to do that. Or lose control and tell her sister just how deep and close had been the relationship between her and Emile. So much closer than any relationship she had ever known before. Yet Emile would probably deny that, and Jane would hate her for it. So what was she going to do?

The answer came to her as she pulled herself stiffly up from the wooden seat where she had been sitting, shivering and stiff with discomfort, because it was then that she noticed the discarded newspaper which had been left behind by someone who was evidently looking for a job. The paper was folded neatly to show a few columns of situations vacant, but a closer glance at those columns showed her that they were not London vacancies, but jobs on offer in places like Leeds or York. It seemed to her then that this copy of the *Yorkshire Post* gave her the solution to her problem, if she had the courage to take it. She would go to Yorkshire, find a job and somewhere to live. That way she would not have to endure living in the same place as Jane, and would not have to suffer the pain of seeing her and Emile together.

The decision made, she felt herself calming

down, and realising that it was time she went back to the bookshop because her father would be worrying about her. She was right about that. He did not attempt to hide his relief when she went in through the back door and joined him in the office.

'Sorry, Dad,' she said, pushing her wet hair away from her face.

'I was getting worried about you,' he admitted. 'It's not like you to blow your top as you did this morning.'

'I just couldn't stand any more from Jane. I had to get away.'

'I know. I understand how you must feel, my dear.' He took her chilled hands in his own warm ones and looked into her face with compassion.

'You'll understand why I have to get right away for a while then, Dad?'

He frowned. 'Where to? Do you mean somewhere for a holiday?'

She shook her head. 'No. I have to get away for longer than that, at least until the wedding is over.'

His frown deepened. 'Where will you go? Have you some place in mind? Some job in mind?'

'No job as yet, but I know where I'm heading for. I've decided to go up to Yorkshire.'

She had clung to that decision all the time since picking up that discarded *Yorkshire Post*. Along with the decision had come memories of holidays spent in North Yorkshire, idyllic days when her mother had been alive and they had been a close, united family staying at Ravensford Manor and exploring the surrounding fells and dales. There had been no problems then, no discord between herself and Jane. She would go back to Ravensford. For surely if there was solace to be found anywhere for her bruised spirit she would find it in that tranquil Pennine village.

Her father seemed to have read her mind. 'Were you thinking of going to Ravensford?'

Carla nodded.

'It might not be the same, you know. The village could have changed. It's a long time since we were there, and you'll be on your own this time with no one to keep you company,' her father warned.

'That's the idea, Dad. To be on my own. To get away from everyone for a while. I must do that — '

He sighed. 'You know best, Carla, but I'll miss you.'

She swallowed. 'I'll miss you, Dad. I expect I'll be back, when I've come to terms with the way things are now.' She knew her decision to go had hurt him.

She waited until the end of that week, by which time her father had found someone to take her place in the bookshop. During that time she saw little of her sister, since Alex Bradley had warned Jane to keep a low profile. They said goodbye quietly, warily, then Carla hugged her father before hurrying out to set her Mini in motion for the journey north.

A curious sense of apathy had settled over her by then, a feeling that it did not much matter what happened to her. Her father had wanted her to book in at Ravensford Manor before leaving, but she had rejected that idea, saying she might stop somewhere on the way as she was so tired. The truth was that she did not want to tie herself down to anything. She wanted to drift along and see what happened. She was just too lethargic to care about the future, even the immediate future.

For hours she drove on monotonous grey motorways, stopping briefly to drink coffee when she knew that her concentration was slipping. Mist was creeping over the landscape by the time she reached North Yorkshire, forcing her to reduce her speed. The mist turned to rain as she left the thundering traffic behind and took a quieter, narrower, country road.

It should not be long before she came to Ravensford, she thought as the fells, crowned with dark clouds, drew closer. Through the village of grey stone houses then and down the long winding hill on the other side. A sharp left turn brought her alongside a stone wall, and there at last was the manor perched on top of a gentle grassy incline. Already some of the lower windows of the gracious old place showed the golden glow of lamps switched on early to disperse the gloom.

Carla spared a passing glance for the neat board which stated that this was Ravensford Manor as she drove between tall gateposts, then sped beneath a line of majestic chestnut trees towards the front door. A moment later she was standing with her finger pressing hard on the bell, since the front door was not standing open, as she recalled it used to do.

She did not have long to wait for the door to open. From inside she heard a male voice call out to someone, 'She's here at last, thank God,' then the heavy piece of carved oak swung back and a man was ushering her inside. The man gave her a long look that held annoyance in its depths, then turned away to speak to someone behind her.

'Go back to bed, Mother. At once,' he said sharply.

Now he turned to Carla again. 'You are very late. I was told you would be here no later than four-thirty.'

Carla stared at him, and took a step backward. 'But I — '

He did not give her time to utter her protest. 'This way, and you'll need to get a move on. They don't like to be kept waiting for their dinner.'

With one hand taking a firm hold of her arm he thrust her ahead of him through the hall and from there ushered her through a door which led, she discovered, into a room she had certainly never entered in her previous visits to the manor. She was standing in a kitchen that was spacious and well-appointed.

Her eyes widened. 'I think there must be some mistake,' she began.

'I haven't time to talk to you now,' the man interrupted. 'I'll have to leave you to get on with it because I've just had an emergency call. Bessie will help you.' I'll see you later.'

'But — ' she began again.

'No time to talk now. I have to go. Bessie will explain things.'

With that the man departed, running a large hand distractedly through a thick thatch of red-brown hair. Carla looked about her, wondering where Bessie was, and if she would be able to make her understand that all she wanted was a room for the night. Then her startled gaze fell on the figure at the other side of the room. A child, was her first thought. Then she saw that the face above the tiny body was that of an elderly woman, and that it was staring at her with some hostility.

'You're late,' the little woman said. 'Doctor David told me you'd be here at half past four. We'll never be ready on time now.'

Carla looked about her at the chaos made by preparations for the cooking of a large meal, looked for the sturdy figure of the man who had thrust her into this unfamiliar room, but the man was out of the house now. She could see him through the picture window of the kitchen climbing into a hefty, Land-Rover type vehicle which was topped by a sign and a revolving lamp. No use looking for help from him since he was involved with a crisis of some sort. Her gaze came back to the woman he had called Bessie, the woman who was scowling at her.

What was it all about? Was she in the middle of a nightmare? Had her brain become unhinged by her weeks of misery?

Two

'Aren't you going to get started, then? It's late enough already,' the tiny woman called Bessie said sharply as Carla gazed about her in bewilderment at the disordered room. 'Mrs Ross put the joint in the oven and I've prepared all the vegetables like I always do, but I can't lift the pans on to the stove and I can't make Yorkshire pudding. Mrs Ross always does that.'

'Is Mrs Ross the cook?' Carla asked, thinking it best to humour the little person.

Bessie chuckled. Her heavy shoulders shook with merriment. 'Oh, that's rich! Is Mrs Ross the cook? You're the cook, Miss. That's why you've come here, isn't it?'

Carla swallowed the words of denial that came to her throat. It was a crazy situation to find herself in when she had only come to the manor to find herself a room for the night, but there seemed to be some sort of crisis happening so she would go along, for the time being, with what seemed to be expected of her. In any case, there was Bessie grumbling at her again.

'The potatoes should have been on twenty minutes ago, if they are going to be roasted. They

20

would have been if Mrs Ross hadn't been taken bad.'

'But I — '

'What made you so late?'

'I had a long way to drive.'

'Well, you're here now, so you'd better get a move on or they'll all be complaining if dinner is late. It won't be my fault. I can't cook dinner for twenty on my own. That's your job.' At that point the puckered face gave Carla a look so fierce that amusement bubbled up inside her.

Well, she had come to Yorkshire in search of a job and now she had got one, without even having to apply for it. She bit her lip as she struggled to contain her laughter.

'What's so funny?' Bessie demanded to know. 'If you were old and not able to look after yourself *you* wouldn't like to be kept waiting for your dinner, would you?'

Carla straightened her face with an effort. 'No,' she agreed, on her way to lift the large pan of potatoes on to the cooker.

She might as well go along with what the little woman, and the man she had addressed as Doctor David, expected of her for this one evening, since she had nothing else to do with her time. No doubt as soon as he came back the doctor would explain to her what it was all about, and in the meantime there was always the chance that the real cook would turn up and take over from her. Of course, it would not be easy, since she had never cooked for such a large number of people, but after her mother's death she had taken over the cooking for her father and for Jane, when she was at home, and sometimes for guests. Jane would have to do that now, she thought wryly, and Jane hated cooking . . .

There was no time to spare after that for thinking of anything except how to have all the vegetables ready, and the Yorkshire puddings cooked at the same time as the beef. The joint proved to be so large that it was difficult to lift from the oven. Bessie certainly would not have managed it, but the delicious aroma of the roasting meat served to remind her of how hungry she was. She had not eaten since early that morning, and then not much, but if she was acting as unpaid cook here at Ravensford Manor she would certainly eat well tonight, she decided as she spooned the batter into individual pudding tins.

'What about the dessert course?' she asked Bessie when these were in a very hot oven, while the beef rested in the warming compartment.

'Mrs Ross made two big trifles before she was taken ill, and there's ice-cream for those who are too fussy to eat that,' came Bessie's forthright reply.

'Who sets the tables, and where?' was Carla's next question.

'The dining room's next door, and the tables were set long before you got yourself here. A bad timekeeper, aren't you? Not like us lot, we're always on cue,' she added proudly.

Carla found herself puzzling over that remark, but would not be drawn into discussion about her bad timekeeping. That could wait until dinner had been eaten.

'Who does the carving?' she asked, knowing it

was something she would find hard to do.

'Doctor David, if he's in. If not, Mrs Ross does it.'

Carla's heart sank. 'But he's not here, and Mrs Ross is ill, isn't she?'

Bessie pulled a face. 'If you can't do it we'll have to ask Mr Peacock to help out, and he'll be boasting for the rest of the night about what a good job he's made of it.'

'Is Mr Peacock one of the residents?'

Bessie nodded vigorously, so that her double chins wobbled. 'Been here for years. The Great Paolo Peacock, Europe's greatest magician, he calls himself. He might have been once, but not any more. He's resting now, like all of us.'

'You mean he's retired now?'

'That's right. Wouldn't be here otherwise, would he?'

'Wouldn't he? I don't quite follow you — '

'All out to grass, aren't we? At least for most of the time. Not many variety theatres left for the likes of us to play in,' Bessie added with a sigh.

'The likes of you, Bessie?' Carla was more puzzled than ever about the setup here at Ravensford Manor.

'Helped a juggler, I did. Until he died. No one else would take me on, so I came here.'

'So you were on the stage at one time?'

''Course I was. We all were, until we got past it. Some of us still do a bit at times, mostly at charity shows, but not me. I just work here.'

'So there are several of you staying in the hotel just now?'

Bessie stared, then shook with laughter. 'The

hotel? You mean the home, don't you?'

Now it was Carla's turn to stare. Words trembled on her lips but before she could voice them there came from within the building a thunderous sound as a massive brass gong was subjected to a thorough beating. She flinched.

Bessie did not turn a hair. 'Jacob's turn tonight to do that,' she grinned. 'Used to be a strong man in a circus.'

'That's not hard to believe,' Carla said as she strained vegetables and put them into dishes already waiting in the warming oven. To her relief the small Yorkshire puddings were well risen and crisp looking. As she piled them into one of the hot containers she heard a car stop in the paved yard outside the kitchen.

'Doctor David's back,' Bessie said with satisfaction. 'So we won't need any help from the great Paolo.'

Carla turned her head as the door opened and saw that the man who had thrust her into this situation was staring at her.

'How's it going?' His voice was terse but not unpleasant.

'Quite well, I think. All ready to serve.'

'Good. I'm starving. You can take it into the dining room and I'll be with you in a moment to do the carving.'

So it was that Carla got her first look at the people for whom she had been cooking, and an intriguing sight they presented as they took their places at the individual tables. Her father would have described them as dressed to the nines, especially the women, who wore mostly quite ornate and colourful afternoon or evening dresses.

Some of the men wore bow ties. All were well turned out. The air was full of their lively talk. Then the man called Doctor David was at Carla's side.

'Perhaps you wanted to do the carving, Miss Crowther? If so, please go ahead.' He smiled at her as he waited for her response.

Carla was horrified at the suggestion. 'Oh no, Doctor. I'd much rather you did it.'

'It must have been part of your catering college course?'

She could not go into her explanation now, not in front of all these old people who were already showing too much interest in her.

'I wasn't very good at it,' she said hurriedly.

Without further comment, he took up the carving knife and fork and proceeded to deal with the large joint of beef speedily and skilfully until everyone was served. Then he turned to Carla and said, with amusement lurking in his hazel eyes. 'I take it that you are prepared to eat what you have cooked, Miss Crowther?'

'Of course, I'm very hungry.' She wondered what he would say when he heard that she was not Miss Crowther.

'Good. You'd better sit with me at the table near the door.'

Carla saw that the table was set only for two. She saw that his plate was well filled and that he ate the food with enjoyment. Apart from passing a brief remark about the tenderness of the meat he did not speak to her until his plate was empty, and her own well on the way to being so. Then his broad, freckled face turned suddenly boyish as he grinned at her.

'You may be a bad timekeeper, Miss Crowther, but you can certainly cook. Even my mother couldn't do any better than you've done today.'

'Thank you.' Should she tell him now, or wait until after he had eaten his trifle? Before she could decide, a plaintive voice sounded from the next table.

'What's for pudding, Miss? I like puddings.'

Before Carla could answer, the doctor did so for her. 'You can wait a moment, Toby, until Miss Crowther has finished her own meal,' he admon-ished the wizened faced little man.

Carla stood up. 'I've finished now. I'll bring in the trifles,' she said with a smile for Toby.

'Would you help by collecting the plates please, Toby?' the doctor asked then. 'We are in a crisis situation just now, with both Mother and Mrs Golightly down with this wretched 'flu. Miss Crowther hasn't had time to settle in yet, so can we all try to help her? I know I can rely on you, ladies and gentlemen, can't I?'

'Oh yes, Doctor. The show must go on,' the old man called Toby replied.

Carla, pushing the trolley full of dishes back into the kitchen, found herself smiling as another frail voice, female this time, broke in, 'Yes, the show must go on. We never close!'

'Millie can't forget that she once used to dance at the Windmill Theatre in London during the war,' Bessie murmured from behind Carla. 'She still likes to do a bit of dancing when we are having a party night, but of course she has to wear a few more clothes now than she did then.'

Carla was still giggling at the idea of Millie, who must be all of seventy years old, scantily clad and dancing behind a feather fan when she entered the dining room again with the huge cut glass bowls containing the trifle.

'You seem to be getting on very well with Bessie,' David Ross said. 'You'll need to if you are to stay here. She doesn't take to everybody,' he added quietly.

Carla wondered what his reaction would be when he heard that she was not the cook he was expecting, and would not be staying. She went on spooning sherry trifle into sundae dishes and tried not to think about that. It would be soon enough for her to confess when the meal was over. At least then if he exploded with anger, as he might well do, she would have finished her meal and be feeling more ready to do battle with him. Because, after all, it was *his* fault she had been forced to cook dinner for all of them. He had been responsible, and she would not hesitate to tell him so, once she had eaten some of the delicious looking trifle.

He was watching with amusement as she savoured every spoonful. Now he spoke. 'My mother certainly knows how to make a good Yorkshire trifle, don't you agree, Miss Crowther?'

She nodded. 'Oh yes, it's gorgeous. I'm sorry she's ill. I don't suppose she is feeling like eating any of this herself?'

'No. All she needs at present are plenty of hot liquids, and medication.'

'Shall I take her a hot drink now?'

'No. Bessie will do it. I don't want you exposed to the virus or we'll soon be without a cook again. It's a particularly nasty thing.' He looked concerned as he told her that.

'Would you like coffee now, Doctor?'

'Yes, please. We'll talk about your hours and conditions of work then. You'll already know about the salary, the agency will have seen to that. Of course, my mother usually deals with everything connected with the paying guests, but she simply isn't well enough to do so at present.'

Carla did not wait to tell him that she knew nothing about the agency from which she had supposedly been recruited. Instead she hurried to the kitchen with her mind in a turmoil of apprehension because very soon now she would have to tell David Ross the truth about her arrival at Ravensford Manor, and she did not know who was going to be the most embarrassed, she or him.

'Come and sit down, Miss Crowther,' he said, after she had poured coffee for everyone. 'You must be ready to take a breather now after all your hard work.'

'Yes.'

She sank into the chair opposite to his and began to sip her coffee while trying to summon up the right words to start explaining things to him. It was ridiculous really, like something out of a television sit-com, the way she had come here looking for a room for the night and found herself landed with the task of cooking for this extended and unusual family. But what had happened to the real cook, the one who was supposed to be here at four-thirty? What had happened to Miss Crowther?

Even as that question teased her mind the answer to it was at hand. It came in the telephone call which took Dr Ross out into the hall. As she waited for him to come back, Carla was able to hear his terse comments through the door behind where she was sitting. A moment or two later he was filling the doorway and there was a deep frown creasing his brow.

'We can't talk here,' he said. 'Will you come into the office? I expect you've got a good explanation to give me. I can't wait to hear it.'

Carla set down her cup with tense fingers. Her guess had been right, that 'phone call had been from the woman who should have come from the agency to cook the meal they had just eaten. She met the doctor's challenging glance with an unflinching stare, then followed him across the hall into a small but comfortably furnished office.

'Sit down,' he ordered.

Carla sat. She would wait for him to start, since it was his fault that she had been dragged into his kitchen in the first place.

'So,' he began when she was seated in one of the pair of armchairs the room held as well as a desk and a filing cabinet. 'Who are you, since you are certainly not Miss Crowther?'

'Carla Bradley.'

'Well, I don't want to sound ungrateful, Miss Bradley, but just how did you manage to find your way into our kitchen?'

She scowled at him. 'I didn't *find* my way into your kitchen, Doctor Ross. You just took hold of me when I came to the door and almost dragged me into your kitchen. You didn't ask who I was, you just assumed that I was the new cook.'

'Why didn't you tell me I was mistaken? Surely it would have been easy enough for you to do that?'

Carla had to laugh at the absurdity of that. 'I tried to tell you but you wouldn't listen to me. You just rushed away and left me.'

He looked startled for a moment. Then, 'Yes, of course. I had to go with the Immediate Care Unit to a farm accident. I suppose my mind was full of that when I opened the door to you. You didn't protest over loudly though when I hurried you into the kitchen.'

'I did,' she argued. 'At least I tried to, but you wouldn't listen. You just told me to get on with it, and since I could see that there was a crisis of some sort going on, what else could I do?'

He chuckled, then his face sobered again. 'You could have walked out, but you didn't, and I'm immensely grateful to you. I owe you an apology too. What were you doing on our doorstep anyway? Were you coming to visit someone here?'

She shook her head. 'No, I came to Ravensford Manor looking for a room.'

'Looking for a room?' He raised a rusty eyebrow. 'Aren't you a little young for a place like this?' Amusement warmed his expression as he said that.

'I didn't know the manor was a place like this. The last time I stayed here it was just an ordinary country house hotel.'

'That must have been some years ago?'

'Yes. I came with my parents a few times when I was in my early 'teens. We all loved it because it was so close to the fells and we liked walking. So when I needed to get away for a while I thought at once of Ravensford, and decided to come here.'

'You didn't think of ringing to book a room before you came?' His glance, resting on her face, was curious.

Carla shook her head. 'No, I was in too much of a hurry to get away.'

Now the frown was back. 'I still can't understand why, after you'd been more or less stampeded into the kitchen and left there with Bessie, you stayed and cooked that magnificent meal for us. Why you didn't just march out again.'

Carla hesitated. 'Perhaps I just didn't know what to do with myself. I came away at short notice, without making any plans. Besides, Bessie was so worried about how she was going to cope. She kept saying how late I was, and that she couldn't lift the big pans herself because she wasn't tall enough. I couldn't just leave her to it.'

His eyes were resting on her with the sort of intent, perceptive look as she guessed he would have given to one of his patients. The silence between them deepened and she became apprehensive again, wondering if he would be angry with her for taking the place of the absent Miss Crowther. If he would be suspicious of her motives.

'What was your real reason for staying?' The question came crisply enough to startle her.

It would have to be the truth, she knew then. 'I was feeling too miserable to care what I did, or what happened to me,' she said in a low voice. 'I don't suppose you believe me, but it happens to be the truth.'

'Do you want to talk about it?'

She shook her head. 'No. I want to leave it

behind, if I can. That's why I came to Yorkshire.'

'From where? The South?'

'Yes. London.'

'Is your home there?'

'Yes. My father has a bookshop there. I help him. At least, I have been helping him — '

'Until you had to get away?'

'Yes.'

His face relaxed. 'Well, you got here just in time to help me over a crisis, so I must thank you for that even if I don't understand your motive for doing it. I'd still have been waiting for Miss Crowther to arrive. She telephoned a few minutes ago to say that she had come via the ford and got her car stuck there, and got so wet wading out that she was forced to go back to Leeds to change her clothes.'

'I saw the ford, but I decided against chancing my ancient Mini through it. It seemed safer to go the long way round, through Ravensley. Now I'd better find my way back down there and get a place for the night, if I can.'

The doctor rose to his feet. 'I think the least I can do, in the circumstances, is to offer you the room Miss Crowther was to have had. It isn't luxurious but it's quite comfortable.'

Carla stood up. 'I'd be glad not to have to drive again tonight. I'm very tired. I haven't been sleeping too well recently.'

'Is that why you decided to take a late holiday?'

'It isn't a holiday. I'm hoping to stay, if I can find a job,' she told him.

'What sort of job?'

'I don't know. Perhaps something to do with the

tourist industry. I might try hotel work. I did some during the long vacations when I was at college and I enjoyed it.'

'How do you feel about cooking?'

Carla smiled. 'I can do it, even on a fairly large scale, can't I? I've been looking after my father since my mother died, and I've learned to enjoy cooking for him, and myself, and sometimes for guests.'

'You'd regularly have about eighteen guests here, plus my mother and myself and sometimes Mrs Golightly. Could you cope with that every day, do you think?'

She stared at him. 'Do you mean until the woman from the agency is able to start work?'

'No, I mean for longer than that. Miss Crowther isn't coming to work here. I don't know whether her experience down in the ford put her off, but she said she feels we are a bit too far out in the wilds for her.'

'That's going to be awkward for you, isn't it?' Carla could not believe he was really offering *her* the job as cook here. If he was, could she do it? Did she want to do it? Extreme tiredness was affecting her judgement so that she felt incapable of making a decision about her future. All she could be sure of was that she wanted a place to sleep.

'Not if you take on the job,' he said quietly.

She hesitated. 'Can I think about it and let you know in the morning, please?'

'Of course. I have rather sprung it on you, and you must be very tired, but I've been worrying about what to do. How to feed all the old dears, since so few of them have any idea of cooking because they've lived in theatrical digs for most of their working lives.'

'You mean, they are all ex-show business people?' Carla was intrigued, in spite of her weariness.

'Yes. Some of them still leave us at times to take part in productions, or for the odd charity concert. They are really great folk. My mother loves having them here, when she is well enough to cope with them. They are such fun, so lively and intelligent. My own life would be poorer without them. But I mustn't keep you standing about here when you are tired. Come, I'll show you to your room.'

He led the way out into the hall and up the stairs to a wide landing where a gallery overlooked the lower floor. Up another flight of steps then to the top floor of the manor, where he opened a white-painted door so that she could see a bed-sitting room which had an adjoining bathroom.

'I hope you'll be comfortable here. We'll talk again in the morning about − ' He broke off abruptly as the 'phone began to ring. 'I'm on call tonight, I'll have to go.'

He turned and ran down the stairs at speed, his bright hair glowing above his tweed clad shoulders. Already he had forgotten her.

A few moments later, when she went downstairs herself to get her suitcase, she heard the sturdy vehicle which held the mobile surgery roar away down the drive. Another emergency, she guessed.

As she went upstairs again with her luggage she met Bessie, who was carrying a hot milky drink into one of the bedrooms. The dwarf grinned at her.

'You'll need to be up early,' she said. 'Doctor David likes his breakfast at eight o'clock prompt. Don't be late this time, will you?'

'I won't,' Carla promised.

Three

Carla woke with a start, all her senses instantly alert, and realised that for the first time in weeks she had slept well. That there had been no lying awake grieving because she had lost Emile to Jane, no tossing and turning because she was dreading having to listen to her sister talking on and on about the wedding.

This morning she would not have to listen to Jane, but there was an ordeal of a different sort awaiting her, the cooking of breakfast not for the three people she was used to cooking for but for nineteen, and since Dr Ross wanted his meal at eight o'clock she had better get up and make a start.

When she had showered and dressed, she crossed to the window and drew back the curtains. She felt her heart lift then with delight as she stared at the sun-drenched landscape, at green lawns stretching down to meet ancient trees, while in the distance the towering fells glowed purple and gold beneath a carpet of bracken and heather. There had been drastic changes at Ravensford Manor since last she had stayed here but the scenery was as glorious as ever. Surely, if she took the job Dr

Ross had offered her last night, she could learn to be contented here, if not happy?

As the thought came into her mind she was distracted by the sound of a sharp whistle, directly beneath her window. She looked down then and saw a sight that brought a smile to her face. A large, black woolly coated dog was attempting to drag what looked like half a tree across one of those smooth stretches of lawn, while Dr Ross, clad in an Arran sweater and a pair of cords, was trying to bring him to heel. As if he sensed that she was watching him, the doctor looked up and gave her a brisk 'Good morning, Miss Bradley.' Perhaps he was thinking that it was time she got on with cooking his breakfast, Carla thought guiltily after a glance at her watch.

Even before she pushed open the door and entered the kitchen she could hear Bessie singing enthusiastically as she set out cups and saucers ready for the serving of early morning tea to the residents. The room was full of sunshine that streamed in through the huge picture window which gave first a view of the paved back court-yard then one of the Pennines. Bessie broke off from her rendering of a wartime ballad to ask Carla if she would like some tea.

'Yes, please, Bessie.' Then, since the little woman had called her Miss Crowther, she added, 'and the name is Carla.'

'That's nice,' Bessie approved as she poured out a mug of a strong brew from a large brown teapot.

'What does the doctor like for his breakfast?' Carla asked after taking a few sips from the mug, and before Bessie could go back to belting out her song.

'Doctor David likes the lot, porridge, bacon and eggs, coffee and toast with marmalade, once he's walked that Figaro. Though it always looks to me as if it's Figaro walking him,' Bessie ended, faintly disapproving.

Carla began to worry. Cooking the bacon and eggs presented no problem, she had done that often enough, but porridge was something she had never cooked. There were bound to be directions on the packet though, she decided as she went into the pantry to find this.

The oatmeal, she discovered, was kept in a large container simply labelled OATS, and with no hint of how these should be cooked. So it would have to be guesswork, or advice from Bessie. She opted for the latter.

'How much shall I make, Bessie?' she asked hopefully during the next lull in Bessie's singing.

'Better make plenty, Carla. Doctor David likes his porridge, and he likes it thick with plenty of honey and cream.'

It was certainly thick, Carla had to admit a few minutes later when she was still trying to smooth out the lumps which persisted in the large steaming pan of cereal. The oats had swelled during cooking so much that there was hardly any space left for the addition of more liquid. As she was worrying about this the big black dog bounded into the kitchen, followed by his master.

'How are things going, Miss Bradley?' the doctor asked.

'It's almost ready, Doctor.'

Bessie had stopped singing and was gazing at

them both for a moment before saying what was in her mind. 'Have I gone funny or something? She was Miss Crowther last night, now she's Miss Bradley. What's going on?'

Carla's lips twitched. Let David Ross explain this one, since he had been responsible for it. She watched, still stirring uneasily the lumpy mixture in the pan, while his features relaxed as he smiled at the dwarf.

'No, Bessie, you've not gone funny. She was Miss Crowther last night. But she is Miss Bradley today.'

Bessie frowned. 'How come? Has she changed her name overnight?'

'No. She never was Miss Crowther. She was only Miss Bradley, and she came here looking for a room for the night just at the time when I was expecting Miss Crowther to arrive. So I bundled her in here and left her with you, and I believe you told her to get on with cooking the dinner because she was late. We didn't know that the real Miss Crowther had got her car stuck in the ford, did we?'

The dwarf exploded into mirth. Her heavy shoulders shook with merriment. 'Oh, Doctor David, just wait till I tell the others about this! You'll never live it down you know.'

He laughed with her. 'I don't suppose I will. Yet it was an easy mistake to make when I *was* expecting a new cook to arrive from the agency in Leeds, and they had said that she was a young woman not long out of Catering College. At least Miss Bradley is young, and she certainly can cook — '

Bessie gave Carla a puzzled stare. 'But what was she doing looking for a room here?'

Now it was Carla's turn to explain. 'Because I'd stayed here before, with my parents. About seven years ago was the last time.'

'Oh, that was before Mrs Ross turned it into a home for us. You'd hardly qualify for a room here now, because I'm the youngest and I'm fifty-nine,' Bessie pointed out, still smiling.

'She has qualified now, because I've offered her the job of cook, if she wants it.'

Carla began to wonder if he would withdraw his offer when he saw the state of the porridge she had made for him. It was more than likely, she thought.

'But what about the other one, the one who should have come?' Bessie was eager to know.

'As I told you, Bessie, she got her car stuck in the ford and had to wade out — '

'Silly bit — ' Bessie began.

'Behave yourself, Bessie! Miss Bradley hasn't made her mind up yet whether or not she wants to stay, and we do need her desperately. So don't put her off.'

'Yes, we do need her, if the other one isn't coming,' Bessie conceded.

'She isn't. She's decided we are too far out in the wilds for her. Too far away from city life.' Dr Ross's face sobered as he said that. 'We've heard it before, haven't we, Bessie?'

'Yes, Doctor David,' the little woman said sadly.

There was a curious atmosphere between the two of them, something Carla was not able to understand as she looked from one sombre face to the other. As though he resented her staring at him, Dr Ross spoke sharply.

'I could do with my breakfast now, if it's ready Miss Bradley.'

'Yes, Doctor.'

As she ladled porridge into a dish Carla wondered what had so abruptly brought about the change in his mood. Something certainly had, and she guessed he would be even more displeased when she gave him his porridge because in spite of all her efforts it was still lumpy. She carried it into the dining room and placed it before him. He did not look up at her but went on reading his newspaper.

'You made a right mess of that, didn't you?' Bessie remarked as she crossed the kitchen to dispose of the remains of the disgusting porridge. 'Doctor David won't like it. You'll need to do better with the bacon and eggs.'

'I'm more used to cooking those,' Carla replied with more confidence than she was feeling as she placed rashers of bacon under the hot grill.

She did not have to wait long for the doctor's reaction. He marched into the kitchen as she was turning the rashers, bearing the full bowl of cereal and with an expression of acute distaste on his features.

'I don't think I can face this, Miss Bradley,' he told her tersely. 'I doubt if even Figaro could stomach it, and he'll eat almost anything. I'll have the bacon and eggs as soon as you can manage it. That's if you *can* manage it.'

Carla's cheeks grew even hotter as she hung on to her temper with an effort, because she had already decided that she was going to accept the job of cook here, at least for the time being. She did not look at David Ross but concentrated on frying a couple of eggs with just sufficient bacon fat to give added flavour. The bacon was crisped to perfection, she saw with relief. As she followed him into the dining room, and put the plate of food before him she did not wait to hear his verdict but hurried back to join Bessie, who was setting a small table in the kitchen for herself and Carla.

'Doctor likes to eat in peace on a morning and read his paper and his post,' she said.

That suited Carla, since the man she had just left was hardly the same man who had spoken so pleasantly to her earlier in the day. She concentrated on what Bessie was telling her about the procedure for serving breakfast to the residents of Ravensford Manor. Some, who were very elderly, took light breakfasts in their rooms, others, mostly men, came downstairs and ate heartily. 'Afterwards you'll have to go and get what you want for lunchtime and tonight's dinner from the village shops and the market garden,' Bessie informed her.

'If I'm still here to cook lunch or dinner,' Carla said ruefully. 'Doctor Ross might have changed his mind about giving me the job.'

'Shouldn't wonder at that, after that bloody awful porridge,' Bessie told her frankly. Then she grinned. 'You'll have to stay and do lunch though 'cos I can't manage on my own. Mrs Ross isn't well enough to help today like she often does. She looked terrible when I took her cup of tea in. No wonder Doctor David's so worried about her.'

Later, when she had finished her own breakfast, Dr Ross came to say that he would like a few words with her in the office.

Carla got to her feet and, aware that Bessie was watching her with open curiosity, went to the room across the hall. Was he about to tell her that he did not wish her to take on the job of cook at Ravensford Manor after all? He motioned her into a chair, but remained standing himself so that he was looking down at her as he put his first question.

'Have you decided yet, Miss Bradley?'

'Decided?'

'About whether or not to take the job as cook here. If you are not going to accept it, I'll have to get on to the agency and ask them to send someone else.'

'You mean — you still want me, in spite of the porridge?'

His mouth curved upwards, his eyes lit with amusement. 'Yes, I still want you, in spite of that dreadful porridge. You can certainly cook bacon and eggs, but we'll cut out the porridge in future. That is, if you are staying on — '

Carla smiled. 'Bessie tells me I *have* to stay on, to cook lunch as there's no one else to do it.'

'We could do with you staying for longer than that. In fact, Miss Bradley, I need your help quite desperately. Because I've no time to interview anyone else and my mother, who usually does that sort of thing, is too ill to be involved. I'll need to get Mother into hospital today, so I'd be much obliged if you would stay and cook for us, even if only temporarily.'

'I'll stay,' Carla promised. 'I might as well do that as anything else, if you are prepared to put up with any mistakes I might make.'

His face sobered. 'Do you have any health problems? The sort of thing that could make it hazardous for you to work here where this particularly nasty virus has got such a hold? You look healthy enough — '

'I am,' she assured him. 'I can't remember when I was last ill.'

'Thank God for that! Because, as I said, I do need someone to keep things going here while my mother is in hospital. This place is her business, you see. Her life, since my father died. I haven't the time to take over the supervision of it, especially now that one of my partners in the practice has gone down with the damned virus. So, do you think you can manage to work without supervision?'

'I managed last night,' she reminded him. 'And I really had been thrown in at the deep end then. If you'll just tell me what to do about ordering and paying for the food I'll need, I think I can cope with the rest. With help from Bessie,' she added.

He frowned at that. 'Bessie can be a help, but she can also be a problem,' he said thoughtfully. 'She's a marvellous little person. There's so much courage in that tiny body, but so much determination too. She will persist in trying to do things that are beyond her, and she can be very bossy. So you'll need to be quite firm with her, for her own sake.'

'I'll do that,' Carla said, though she knew enough already of Bessie's strong character to guess that it wouldn't be easy.

'I'm sure you will.' He paused, then went on. 'It will be a heavy responsibility for you though, and very different from what you've been used to in your family bookshop. I don't know that I'm being fair in asking you to take it on.'

'What else can you do but take a chance on me and leave me to it?' she asked, stung by the way he had referred to her work in the family bookshop as if there were never any problems there. Never any difficult customers there.

'As you say, what else can I do, since the next applicant from the agency might also decide that we are too far off the beaten track for her and that there will be nothing for her to do in her free time. Will that bother you?'

Carla smiled. 'I don't expect to have much spare time in the next few days.'

He gave her a rueful, attractive grin. 'No, but I'll make it up to you as soon as we are over this crisis. In the meantime, order anything you need from the village grocer or the baker and the butcher. There's only one of each in the village but they are all very good. They'll be able to advise you about quantities et cetera and they'll send in their bills as usual at the end of the month. The vegetables we get from the market garden run by the Muirs, which is out on the Ravensbridge road but within walking distance of here. I know Mother likes to walk down there sometimes if the weather is fine, but you can telephone and they'll deliver. I'll have to leave you now because the ambulance is here to take my mother to hospital. I'll be in for a quick bite to eat sometime in the day, I hope. I'm sure you'll do your best, Miss Bradley.'

'Yes, of course. I hope your mother is soon feeling better, Doctor Ross.' As she said this, Carla prepared to leave him.

'So do I. I'm worried about her, but don't tell the old people, please. They will only be alarmed.'

Two ambulancemen carrying a stretcher passed Carla as she hurried through the hall to rejoin Bessie, who was now full of gloom.

'Mrs Ross is very bad. She couldn't even drink the tea I took her, and she always likes her early morning tea. I'm worried — '

'Doctor Ross doesn't want the others to know that, Bessie. So shall we keep it to ourselves and save them from worrying?' she suggested.

Bessie's frown deepened. 'Some of them will have seen the ambulance, and they are bound to be worried about Mrs Ross.'

'They must be very fond of the doctor's mother.'

'It isn't just that. It's what would happen to us all if anything happened to Mrs Ross.' Bessie's eyes were anxious as she spilled out her fears to Carla. 'We aren't just a lot of old "has beens" to her. We are people who've travelled all over the world to entertain other folk. Some of us have been famous in our day, others only bottom of the bill, but Mrs Ross treats us all as if we are special people still and we need that. It's important to us.'

'I'm sure it is, Bessie,' Carla told her gently. 'But I expect breakfast is important to you too, and it's nearly nine o'clock so we mustn't be late with it.'

Bessie brushed that aside. 'Oh they are not so

punctual about coming down to breakfast, Carla, as they are to dinner. Not used to getting up early, see, after working late at the theatre. Old habits die hard you know, and Mrs Ross has always been easy going about it. They'll come down when they are ready.'

It was shortly after the ambulance had left, followed by Dr Ross on his way to the Health Centre in the village, that the residents began to make their way downstairs for breakfast. Some of them had seen the departure of the ambulance and were swift to voice their concern for their hostess, and for themselves.

'Who'll look after us if Mrs Ross isn't here?' asked an elderly man whose hands, once so skilled at juggling, were now swollen with arthritis.

'I'll look after you, with a bit of help from Bessie,' Carla told him with what she hoped was an encouraging smile.

He stared at her for a moment, frowning, then spoke his mind. 'But you're only a bit of a lass. What do you know about folk like us? We're not like other people, you know. We're special, Mrs Ross says. We've given all our lives to the public entertainment and now it's our privilege to rest, Mrs Ross says. I bet you don't even know what that word means to us, do you, Miss?'

Her smile deepened. 'Oh but I do, Mr — ?'

'Joe. Joe Jefferson, who once performed for royalty,' he told her proudly.

'Really, Joe? And how marvellous for you. I do know what resting means to you, because my father is very interested in the theatre and we often have stage people coming into our bookshop in London, when *they* are resting.'

His face lit up. 'Come from London, do you? I've spent some happy times there, when I was younger. Before this damned arthritis got hold of me. What made you come up here to work, a bright young thing like you? You won't find much to do with yourself up here,' he added. 'Except listen to old fools like me moaning.' With that he gave her a piercing glance from beneath jutting eyebrows which made her decide that she liked this forthright old man.

'I won't have much time to do anything except work until Mrs Ross comes out of hospital, will I Joe?' she told him with a warm smile.

'How long do you think she'll be away?' he asked anxiously.

'I don't know, but as I said, I've promised to look after all of you until she comes home. Now, what are you going to have for your breakfast, Joe?'

Joe's anxiety was shared by all the residents at Ravensford Manor, Carla was to discover as she spoke to them at intervals during that first long and difficult day. Although they were all paying guests here, except for Bessie, who was an employee, the manor had become a real home to them. For many who had spent most of their lives moving from one theatrical lodging to another it was the first settled home they had known in adult life, and they were greatly afraid that with Mrs Ross in hospital the contentment and comfort they had found at Ravensford might suddenly come to an end.

For all of that first day, in between preparing the light luncheon and the evening dinner, making mid-morning coffee and afternoon tea, Carla was aware of the undercurrent of fear that lay only just beneath the surface of their gossip in the dining room, the lounge and the television room. When she carried in hot drinks she noticed that they watched her with wary eyes, not yet able to accept that she would at least try to look after them as well as Mrs Ross always did. When Dr Ross returned briefly to the house for a snack she mentioned their uneasiness.

'It's only to be expected, I suppose,' he answered thoughtfully. 'Mother has devoted all her life to them since my father died. She's worrying as much about them, and how they'll manage without her. Especially as Mrs Golightly isn't here just now.'

'Mrs Ross is certain to be apprehensive, having to leave only Bessie and me to cope with things in her absence. I mean, she never even met me before she was taken into hospital, did she?' Carla pointed out.

'She ought to have been in hospital earlier. For days she wasn't well enough to be on her feet, but because Mrs Golightly was ill she wouldn't stay in bed as I begged her to do. Mother is an asthma sufferer, you see. It was that which put a stop to her own musical career.'

'Was that why she started this place?' Perhaps she ought not to have asked that, Carla thought when it was too late.

'No. She and my father took it over as a hotel. It was after he died that she didn't know whether she could bear to carry on alone. Then Miss Clare, who is a retired opera singer, came to stay along with Mavis, who used to be her dresser. Another friend of Miss Clare's came soon afterwards, with her husband, for a long "rest". Gradually, as they spread the word, others came to join them until my mother found herself with an extended theatrical family. Some of them idolise her, so they are frightened both for her sake and their own. Because this place is home to them now in every sense of the word.'

'But they have you here too. It's your home as well, isn't it, Doctor?'

For a moment he looked startled, taken aback. As though she had said something he did not expect. Then he answered her, and it seemed to her that the answer came with reluctance.

'No, Miss Bradley. This isn't my home. I'm only here temporarily.'

'Oh, I'm sorry — I thought — ' She was confused by both his words and his way of expressing them.

'You were not to know. There's been no time to explain everything to you, and there's still no time because I have more patients to see before I go back to the cottage hospital. You seem to be coping with things here, so I'll leave you to it.'

When he had gone, Carla left Bessie to begin preparations for afternoon tea while she went in search of the market garden where Dr Ross had told her she could buy the vegetables she needed for the evening meal. He had said it was within easy walking distance and the things she required were not heavy, so she decided to go there on foot.

The directions David Ross had given her were easy enough to follow and the walk in bright sunshine through the tree-studded parkland was enjoyable for most of the way, until suddenly, and without any conscious thought of him on her part, she was remembering walking with Emile through one of the famous London parks. All that day she had kept thoughts of Emile at bay simply by being too busy, too involved with her new duties at the manor. Now she was away from the house and the job, and she was back to remembering Emile. Back to desolation because she had lost him.

Was it always to be like this? Was she never to be able to think of him without anguish? If so, her future looked bleak. Yet was he worth spoiling her life for, this man who had promised her so much, and so speedily forgotten his promises when her more glamorous sister came on the scene? No, he was not, and she would not go on breaking her heart over him. She would be angry with him instead because how could you go on loving someone against whom you had a consuming, furious anger? Yet anger brought tears just as surely as did sorrow, Carla discovered in those moments when fury against Emile and against all men built up inside her. Because of the tears and the rainbow coloured mist they brought to her eyes she did not see the rabbit hole that was immediately in front of her feet until it was too late and she was pitching forward to fall on her knees on the rough path that skirted the market garden.

The tears came in real earnest then, tears of shock, frustration and despair. She cried as she had not been able to cry in the flat above the bookshop because her father's bedroom was next to hers and she did not want to distress him. In this quiet and lonely place there was no one to hear. No one to care.

Yet the sound of her sobbing was carried by the breeze over the stone wall that enclosed the market garden, along the rows of shrubs and standard roses to the man who paused with an insecticide spray in his hand and drew his brows together in a frown. For a moment he stood quite still, listening. Then he put down the spray, and began to hurry along the row of scented roses until he came to the wall. Once there, he swung his tall, lithe frame over it and stared down at Carla.

'You're hurt,' he said as he bent over her.

'No,' she mumbled.

'You must be, since you are crying,' he reasoned.

Carla looked up and saw black hair and dark eyes set in a deeply tanned face that was long and lean. There was just enough of a likeness in that face to Emile. A fresh rush of fury enveloped her.

'Go away,' she cried. 'I told you I'm not hurt. Go away!'

Four

'Would you like to tell me what it's all about now?'

Carla looked up, startled, at the man who was leaning on the wall. The man she was sure had walked away from her a few minutes ago after being told quite rudely to do just that. 'I thought — ' she began.

'Yes, you thought I'd gone away, as you suggested I should.'

Now she felt uncomfortable, knowing that he had only tried to help. 'I fell, got my foot stuck in a hole at the side of the path. I didn't even see it — '

'Rabbits. This place is thick with the damned things, and they can clear a row of outdoor lettuce in no time at all.'

'Rabbits?' She felt stupid, trying to understand what he was talking about while her swollen eyes had such difficulty in focusing on him.

'You put your foot down a rabbit hole and went headlong. No wonder you are shaken. You'd better come along to the farm shop and let us give you first aid,' the man said as calmly as if she had not just been so rude to him.

'I was going there anyway,' she muttered, 'until I came to grief.'

'You do need to watch out for the rabbit holes around here,' he said wryly. 'As I said, there are too many of them.'

'And I wasn't watching out,' she admitted. 'I was thinking of something else.'

'Obviously!'

Carla was on her feet now and the man who had come to help was picking up her shopping bag and tucking it under his arm. 'You'd better lean on me,' he said as he noticed her limping.

She was glad of his support as he guided her along the rest of the footpath and in through open gates to a large prefabricated building which had been made into a farm shop. Once in there he urged her into a chair and told her to wait until he came back with the first aid box.

While he was away she looked about her at the colourful displays of choice fruit and vegetables, the cut flowers and pot plants, then he was back with the box and a small bowl of warm water.

'There's no need,' Carla began then as embarrassment flooded her because this strange man was about to bend over the remains of her tights and her badly grazed knee in order to clean up the mess.

'I'll do it Robin,' a female voice interrupted. 'You go and make some tea. She looks as if she needs it.'

The man did not argue with the woman, and did not come back until the knee had been cleaned up and covered with sticking plaster dressing. In his hands as he joined the two girls was a tray supporting three mugs of tea. He handed the first of these to Carla.

'Are you feeling better now?' he asked after she

had swallowed some of the hot liquid.

She nodded. 'Yes, much better, thanks. I'm sorry to have been such a nuisance.'

He gave her an attractive, lopsided grin. 'Think nothing of it. We like to look after our customers, don't we, Morag? By the way, Morag is my sister.'

There was a likeness between the brother and sister. Both were tall and very slender, both had black hair and very dark grey eyes. The sister was within a year or two of being the same age as Carla, the brother some years older than them both.

'But you must have things to do and I'm stopping you from getting on with them, aren't I?'

He grinned at her again. 'You couldn't have timed your arrival better. This is our quietest time of the day. The time we always stop for a drink anyway.' He paused, then went on, 'You must be new around here. We haven't seen you before, have we?'

'No. I only came up here yesterday. I'm at Ravensford Manor.'

This brought a burst of laughter from him. 'You're a bit young for that, surely?' he suggested.

'I'm the new cook there,' she explained with a smile.

'A bit young for that as well, aren't you?' he teased.

'No,' she said defensively. 'At least, I don't think so. I was on my way here to buy some vegetables when I put my foot down the rabbit hole.'

It was Morag who spoke next. 'We were wondering if all was well at the manor, because Mrs Ross hasn't been down to buy anything for two or three days, or even phoned to ask us to send any stuff for her.'

'Mrs Ross is ill. She was taken into hospital this morning, and the cook they had seems to have left earlier in the week. Even the housekeeper is down with 'flu at the moment,' Carla told her.

'Poor David. How will he cope with all the old dears on his own, I wonder?' Morag was looking thoughtful now. 'He'll be up to his eyes in the practice as well, because one of the other doctors has this rotten 'flu. Perhaps I'll give him a ring and see if I can help.'

Her brother's voice was sharp as he answered her. 'I don't think that's such a good idea, Morag.'

Morag put down her mug with a clatter. 'That'll be up to me, won't it Rob? I'm not a child any more, to be told what to do − '

'No, I keep forgetting that,' he said shortly. 'All the same − '

Carla got to her feet, uncomfortably aware of the tension which had suddenly banished the earlier feeling she had had that this brother and sister were on good terms with each other and working in harmony.

'I'll have to be getting back or I'll be late with dinner,' she said hastily. 'If I could just have the things I need − '

Immediately then Robin took his attention away from his sister and gave it all to Carla, while Morag collected the empty mugs and carried them away on the tray. Soon Carla was choosing the snowy white cauliflowers and tiny baby carrots which would be a perfect complement for the chickens she intended to roast that evening. A few pounds of Bramley apples with which to make a crumble for pudding completed her purchases.

'I'll drive you home,' Robin Muir told her then.

'There's no need. I'm quite able to walk, thanks. I've taken up more than enough of your time already.'

'Nonsense!' He gave her that teasing grin again. 'As I told you earlier, we like to look after our customers. Especially — '

'Especially those from the manor,' said Morag, who had just rejoined them. As she spoke, she gave her brother a meaningful glance.

Carla wondered what it was all about. 'As I said, I can manage — '

'You won't make very good speed with your injured leg and that heavy bag, and you don't want to be late with the meal if it's only your second day as cook at the manor, do you?' Robin pointed out.

Carla gave in then. 'No.' She turned to Morag. 'Thanks for all your help. I expect I'll be down tomorrow for some more stuff. I enjoyed the walk, until I fell into the rabbit hole.'

A very few minutes later she alighted from Robin Muir's estate car at the back entrance of Ravensford Manor. Robin followed with the bag of vegetables, straight into the kitchen as though he knew his way. Bessie, who was preparing potatoes at the kitchen sink, greeted him with delight.

'We haven't seen you for ages, Robin. We've missed you. Why didn't you come to play for us?'

He laughed, but it was not an easy laugh, Carla thought. 'Because we've been very busy down at the market garden, Bessie. I haven't had any spare time.'

'You can't be busy *all* the time,' she objected.

'We have been, Bessie. We have to get as much done as we can during the long light evenings you know, and it doesn't leave time for anything else.'

'Well, it's getting darker again now, so you won't have that excuse for neglecting us, will you?' she said sternly.

'No, Bessie,' Robin answered meekly. Then, as he made for the door, he gave Carla a teasing smile. 'You'll need to watch Bessie. She's a bully, you know.'

Carla smiled back. 'I know.'

'Watch out for those rabbit holes too, in future, won't you?'

'I will,' she said with a laugh.

'I'll be seeing you. You too, Bessie.'

With that, he departed. Carla took off her jacket and prepared to help Bessie with the meal.

'He's lovely, isn't he?' Bessie sighed.

'Who?' Carla looked at the tiny woman blankly, her mind full of nothing but how much butter, sugar and flour she would need to weigh out for the crumble topping.

'Robin Muir, of course,' Bessie responded. 'Didn't you think he was very handsome, Carla? You must have done — '

'I didn't really take much notice of what he looked like.' She had only thought, when she first set eyes on him as he bent over her to ask if she was hurt, how much he resembled Emile. Later, while drinking tea at the market garden, she had revised that opinion and decided that his face was much leaner and harder than Emile's, just as his body was more slender and tougher looking. She pushed Emile out of her thoughts with an effort and tried to concentrate on what Bessie was saying to her.

'Didn't take much notice! A girl of your age, when the best looking man for miles around leaves his business to drive you home! You must be — '

'I'm not interested in men,' Carla broke in, 'whether they are good looking or not. All I'm interested in is my job.'

Bessie gave her a stare of disbelief. 'You must be joking! A pretty girl like you!'

'I'm not. I've finished with men. None of them are to be trusted. And I didn't want Robin Muir to drive me back but he insisted, just because I had put my foot down a rabbit hole when I wasn't looking where I was going on my way down to their place, and fell flat on my face.'

Instantly then, Bessie was all concern. 'Did you hurt yourself?'

'I grazed my knee,' Carla looked down at her ruined tights and pulled a face. 'I'll have to change these before we serve dinner.'

'You'd best let Doctor David take a look at that knee as well when he gets back. There might be gravel in it,' Bessie worried.

'There's no need. It's nothing. I'm sure I could have walked back, only the man from the market garden insisted on bringing me.'

'We've missed seeing him. I wondered why he didn't come any more. If it was anything to do with the gossip, because he used to come often enough before Mrs Ross went off to America, to play the piano for us.'

Carla, busy mixing crumble, gave her a questioning look. 'Who looked after this place when the doctor's mother was in America?'

'Doctor's mother didn't go to America. I didn't say that. It was Doctor David's wife who went there. Spoilt little madam,' she added. 'Most of us were glad to see the back of her, though he took it hard.'

'Is he staying here because she's away? Or did they always live here?' Why had she asked that, Carla wondered.

'They didn't live here. That wouldn't have done, because Mrs Ross didn't like her. They lived in the Ford House, just the two of them. He came back after she left because it was easier for him, Mrs Ross said, than keeping his own house going.'

'How long has she gone for?' It must be hard for the doctor, having to cope with this crisis in the absence of his wife, Carla thought as she mixed a savoury stuffing for the poultry.

Bessie paused in the act of slicing apples and took her time about answering that question. 'It's anybody's guess, how long she's gone for, and it's anybody's guess whether she'll ever come back here. I couldn't care less, myself. She was always moaning about it being too quiet here, and wanted the doctor to go and work in one of those big American hospitals where there's plenty of money to be earned. He didn't want that though. Said he was happy here. Next thing we knew, they'd had a big row and she had taken herself off to America on her own.'

'How awful for him,' Carla said, since Bessie obviously expected her to say something.

'Shouldn't have married her anyway! Not when there was someone here he could have had. Only it happened very suddenly, according to our Mrs Ross, while he was working at a hospital in America for a year.'

Bessie's disclosures were brought to an abrupt end by the arrival in the back courtyard of the doctor's car.

'I'll have to run upstairs and change my tights,' Carla said hurriedly. She could not face the doctor yet, so soon after hearing all the sad details of his troubled marriage. If he came into the room now he might guess that she and Bessie had just been talking about him, and be embarrassed. In her own present highly emotive state she felt ultra sensitive to his feelings, and glad to escape to her room for a few minutes.

He was waiting for her when she came down, standing in the hall and on the look out for her. He looked tense and had smudges of fatigue beneath his eyes. 'How are you managing?' he asked without preamble. 'Are you going to be able to cope, do you think?'

Pity for him welled up inside her. He must be under a tremendous strain at present, being responsible for the welfare of all these old people and at the same time having extra work to do in the medical practice he shared with two other country doctors.

'Yes, I can cope. Please don't worry about me,' she told him.

His face lightened, momentarily. 'Good girl! I had a feeling you would be able to cope, though I'm never quite sure how much one should trust

such feelings.' His eyes filled with shadows again
as he said that.

Was he thinking of the wife whose feelings he
had once been so certain of, she found herself
wondering.

'Is there any improvement in Mrs Ross?' she
asked then.

'Not yet. I've just come back to take another look
at Miss Clare and Mavis as they weren't too well
this morning, then it's back to the Health Centre
for me. Don't keep dinner waiting for me. Just save
something that will hot up in the microwave when
I get back. Though heaven knows what time that
will be.'

'I'll do that, Doctor. Have you time to stop for a
hot drink now?'

He smiled tiredly. 'Bessie already had one organised for me. Are you getting on all right with
her?'

She smiled back. 'Yes, I think so. She's getting
me organised, too.'

His eyes showed amusement. 'Well, don't let her
overdo it. She can be a bossy little person, but she
means well.'

'Yes, I know.'

He left her then to check on his two elderly
patients, while Carla went back to her cooking.

As she worked, Carla found her thoughts lingering on the young doctor whose problems were so
enormous that they made her own troubles look
quite trivial. How much worse it would have been
for her if she had married Emile before discover-
ing that he preferred her sister. While she was still
reflecting on this the doctor came back into the

kitchen to drink the coffee Bessie had made for him and to snatch a hasty sandwich.

'Will you take some soup and pudding up to Miss Clare and Mavis instead of dinner, please Bessie?' he asked. 'Jacob and Joe have promised to give you a hand with clearing the tables and anything else you need.' He looked appealingly at Carla then. 'How are you on dog walking, Miss Bradley?'

'Dog walking?' Her voice betrayed her surprise at the question. She was not sure what he was getting at. 'I've never done any. We've never had a dog, with living in a flat in London.'

He studied her silently for a moment, while chewing the last of his sandwich. 'Well, you don't have to be trained for it, but then it's not strictly speaking part of the cook's job either. What I'm trying to ask is, could you manage to give my dog a short walk if I don't get back in time to do so?'

'Yes, of course.'

'But what about — ' Bessie began, glancing at her leg.

'I'll be glad of some fresh air, when I've finished cooking,' Carla broke in before she could say any more. 'Where is the dog?'

'He's in the conservatory at the side of the house, and he's fretting for my mother. Joe and Jacob have both offered to take him, but I think he'll be too strong for either of them. Joe's hands are crippled and Jacob doesn't see too well nowadays. So if you could help — '

'I'll be glad to help,' Carla said, even though she felt nervous as to how she would control that large black dog.

'Thanks. I'll leave you to it then.' With that, David Ross hurried out to his car.

'You shouldn't have said you'd do that. You'll have trouble with that big black brute,' Bessie warned as the car roared away. 'He's wild. I don't know why Doctor David kept him.'

'Perhaps he wanted a big dog?' Carla suggested as she stirred the gravy.

'I don't know that he wanted any sort of dog, but this big black brute turned up on his doorstep the day after his wife left, and he said he'd keep it till the owner turned up. Only the owner never has turned up. I reckon someone just let the big daft thing loose on the moor and drove away. You'll need to watch him or he'll have you off your feet,' Bessie forecast darkly.

The rest of Bessie's gloomy predictions were lost in the thundering of the dinner gong, but later Carla saw what she meant, when, after the meal was over, she reached the conservatory with an anorak on her back and strong shoes on her feet. Luckily, she had the good sense to close the door after her before Figaro flung himself at her and almost knocked her over. Only the door kept her upright. As it was, she reeled beneath the impact of the huge paws, and felt a large warm tongue come out of a laughing mouth to lick her ear.

'Figaro!' she gasped. 'Get down, you great idiot! Sit *down*.' To her amazement, Figaro sat and stared at her with his big brown eyes full of puzzlement because she and not his beloved master was clipping on his lead. Once this was done he was full of devilment again, all his restless energy ready to be spent in leading this stranger a dance. She would keep him on the lead, she decided when she realised how boisterous he was. It would not do to give him his freedom, as his master would have done, because she might not manage to get him back again. So she let him drag her along the path that led away from the house and towards an area of woodland behind it. Already she could understand why David Ross would not allow either Joe or Jacob to take on this task. She was young and fit, but it took all her strength to hold Figaro back as he sped towards the high retaining wall which enclosed the grounds of the manor. All she could do was to hang on and try to keep pace with those elongated black legs that must be part setter, part Labrador and follow that wildly waving black tail as Figaro tore on and on, taking her with him and barking joyously every now and then.

All of a sudden, she was not with him. He was away on his own dragging the chain and leather lead behind him and filling the air with his excitement as he raced away from her and headed for freedom. As she called to him to come back he gave her a laughing backward glance and took the wall in one wild leap.

'Damn!' Carla said with great feeling. An answering bark came from the other side of the wall, and a receding bark at that. She would have to follow him over the wall, or lose him. She followed him, and ruined another pair of tights in doing so, but at least she could see him again.

He was going in the direction of the ford. Going for a swim, she guessed, and that was all she needed at the end of this traumatic day because she'd never manage to get him out of the water without getting soaked herself.

'Damn,' she said again, with even more feeling. 'I must have been mad to let myself in for this. Come here, Figaro!' she shouted, without much hope that he would obey.

Already he was in the water, but he did not stay there. He was out on the other side and taking a flying leap over another wall, this time one that encircled a smaller dwelling than the manor.

'Figaro,' she cried despairingly as she saw her chances of catching him diminishing. Her alarm grew when she noticed the sheep grazing on the hill behind the house. She could imagine the havoc he would create if he found his way into the flock.

He was not interested in the sheep though, she saw as she raced across the footbridge that crossed the ford. In fact, he was waiting at the front door of the beautiful house which must have been built since she had played here as a child, waiting as though he expected at any minute that someone would open the door and let him in. He was raising a paw to scratch at the door as she reached the wrought iron gate and pushed it open. A great surge of relief took possession of her then as he stayed there, waiting for her.

'You're a bad dog,' she scolded as she fastened her fingers firmly round the lead which was still wet from having trailed through the water of the ford with him.

He whined, and pulled her to the door, a modern patio door, which would open on to a paved terrace where stone pots of geraniums flowered with pink and scarlet blooms. She caught a glimpse then of a lovely, elegantly furnished room before turning back with the dog towards the gate. It was then that Figaro heard a familiar car engine and began to bark madly as it came to a halt.

Carla's eyes widened as she recognised David Ross getting out of the vehicle and coming towards her. He was scowling.

'Oh, it's you. I saw someone, trying to get in, I thought, as I came down from the farm. I'd be obliged if you'd keep away from here in future. This place is private. It doesn't belong to the manor. Is that clear?'

Five

Carla felt her neck beginning to burn as she heard the reproof in the doctor's voice. He must think she had come here to pry into his private life, since this house, she now knew, was the Ford House. Well, she wasn't going to let him get away with that.

'I only came here to get Figaro back. I certainly don't make a habit of trespassing on other peoples' property, I can assure you, Dr Ross,' she told him.

He either did not believe her or he was in too much of a hurry to listen to her explanation. Already he was back in the driving seat and turning his car round in the drive of The Ford House before taking it back up the hill.

Figaro gave a disgruntled whine because he had been left behind, and a tug at his lead as though he would like to have followed his master. Carla held on to him with difficulty.

'Behave yourself, Figaro,' she said crossly. 'You've caused enough trouble for me already.'

It seemed to take her a long time to walk back to Ravensford Manor, with the dog accompanying her reluctantly and casting glances back at his old home all the way. She felt tired and discouraged, resentful too of the way David Ross had spoken to her. He could take his own dog out in future, she decided as she made her way back to the house in the gathering dusk.

Yet, later that evening, when the doctor returned from making his final calls of the day, he was again the pleasant, courteous man she had taken him to be earlier. He smiled at her when she carried in the meal she had re-heated in the microwave oven, and apologised for causing her to work so late.

'It won't often happen,' he promised. 'The circumstances are rather exceptional just now.'

'It doesn't matter, I have nothing else to do with my time.' Carla turned away from him, disconcerted by the abrupt change in his manner since their encounter at the Ford House. Weren't all men the same though, blow hot, blow cold, as the mood took them? Like Emile, telling her one week that he loved her, the next week falling for her sister . . .

'Carla, come back a minute,' his voice recalled her as she was about to close the dining room door.

'Yes, Doctor?' She looked at him enquiringly.

'What happened to your leg? Did that damned dog of mine pull you over?'

'Oh no! It was nothing to do with Figaro, and it's only a graze anyway.'

'All the same, you'd better take the dressing off and let me look at it when I've finished my supper.'

'It doesn't need attention, thank you. Goodnight, Doctor,' she added hastily.

She was aware that she had been ungracious to

him, and that his eyes were resting speculatively on her as she left the room, but she was too tired and bewildered by the events of the day to care what he thought of her. She would stay and see him through the immediate crisis and then move on to somewhere where the atmosphere was less emotive.

The days that followed were full of hard work for her as she coped with all the cooking and some of the housework for Dr Ross and his extended family. At first an uneasy atmosphere lay over everyone as the condition of the doctor's mother gave rise to more anxiety and the older residents grew fearful about their future.

Carla tried to reassure them, but her attempts to allay their fears collapsed when two of the old ladies took a taxi to the cottage hospital in order to visit Mrs Ross and were told that she was too ill to receive visitors. Nothing could convince them then that the worst was not about to happen. Neither was David Ross available to calm them. He was out of the house for most of the time. So the mood of depression deepened, and even Bessie no longer raised her voice in her favourite popular ballads as she worked with Carla in the kitchen.

On her daily visit to the Muirs' market garden one afternoon to buy fruit and vegetables, Carla found herself talking about her worries to Robin Muir over a mug of tea.

'It isn't just that the old dears are worried about Mrs Ross because they are so fond of her,' she tried to explain. 'They are terrified of what will happen to them if she dies. They are afraid they might all be split up and have to find fresh homes among strangers who don't understand them. Even Bessie is very quiet and depressed. She doesn't even try to boss me, or Joe or Jacob, around like she did when I first arrived. Nothing I can say will convince her that Mrs Ross will get better and come home one day. Of course, I'm not even sure myself that things will work out like that. I wish I were, Robin,' she ended sadly.

Robin set down his empty mug and rested his eyes on her face thoughtfully. 'I wonder if I could help you?' he asked slowly.

'You? In what way? You have plenty to do here in your own business — ' She stared at him, frowning, not sure of what he was getting at.

'Help you to lift their spirits, I meant. I could come up one evening and play the piano, so they can have a party night, as they call it. Nothing elaborate, just a sing-song really. I've done that a few times before, at Mrs Ross's request, and they seemed to enjoy it.'

'Can none of them play the piano?'

'Strange as it may seem, no. One or two could, before they became victims of arthritis, and Mrs Ross certainly doesn't. The piano belonged to her husband.'

'Would you really give up an evening for them, Robin? I'm sure it would cheer them up. When could you come?'

'Is tonight too soon? Do you need more notice than that?'

'No. Tonight would be marvellous, because it's beginning to get me down listening to all their doom and gloom.'

'Can't David Ross reassure them?' Robin asked then.

Carla considered that, thought of David Ross's weary eyes and the frown which was never far away from his brow; the hurried meals and the speedy departures sometimes even before the meal was finished: the way she found herself taking Figaro out more and more often because his master was too busy. And the way, even when he was at home, David Ross seemed to be totally withdrawn into himself so that he was hardly aware of what was going on and did not even see her as she served his meals or gave him messages.

'I think perhaps Dr Ross needs someone to reassure *him*,' she said slowly. 'He looks so tired sometimes that I don't think he knows what is going on at the manor.'

'He's lucky to have you there to help out. It wouldn't be everyone's choice to be shut up there all day with a house full of people who must be three times your age.'

A long, perceptive glance as he spoke, made Carla feel that Robin was probing into her motives for being at Ravensford Manor. What would he think if he were to discover that she had never intended to become the cook there, that she had been literally dragged into the place by David Ross and left to muddle through as best she could? This last thought brought a faint smile to her lips.

'Oh, I like most of the old people, especially Bessie,' she told him.

'I love Bessie, she's such a character,' he agreed.

'She's rather fond of you — '

He chuckled. 'In that case, I'll certainly come up

and play for her tonight. Shall we say about eight
o'clock?'

'Yes, and thanks a lot, Robin. It will give them
something to look forward to, and cheer them up.'

'It'll give *me* something to look forward to, too,
Carla. The chance to see a bit more of you. You
seem always to be in a hurry to get back. I've been
wanting to ask you for days − '

Panic rose in Carla. So she had not misinter-
preted the looks he had been sending in her
direction at times when Morag had not been
around. She got to her feet from the stool where
she had been perching.

'I'm in a hurry to get back today, Robin,' she told
him, 'especially now you are coming up tonight.
I'll have to get dinner over a bit earlier than usual,
so I must be off.'

She gathered up the bags of vegetables and fruit
she had chosen, anxious to be away before Robin
could finish saying what he had started. He was
nice, but she did not want any complications. It
was too soon for her to take another man into her
life. She had not got over the last one yet . . .

'I'll see you tonight,' she called over her shoulder to him.

He laughed. 'There's no need to panic. I won't
rush you. I'll just be around, when you are ready.'

There was no answer she could make to that, so
she strode briskly away from the market garden,
glad of the cool September air to take the warmth
from her cheeks.

Back at Ravensford Manor, she lost no time in
telling Bessie that her hero was to visit them that
evening to provide some music. Delight flooded

the little woman's features.

'That's just what we all need, a good sing-song. Miss Clare said Robin would never come to play for us again now Mrs Ross isn't here, but I told her she was wrong. I can't wait to see her face when she gets to hear about it. I'll go and tell her now.'

'Will you tell everyone that we'll have dinner fifteen minutes earlier tonight as well, Bessie, please? I want to be all cleared away and ready for when Robin comes.'

'I'll tell them,' Bessie said happily.

The atmosphere in the dining room that evening was livelier than it had been in recent days. Lethargy and anxiety took a back seat for once as the old people tackled plates of steak and kidney pie with renewed appetites. The two elderly gentlemen who had undertaken to collect the empty plates moved jauntily about their duties while Bessie filled the dishwasher and Carla served fresh fruit salad and whipped cream. Dr Ross arrived while they were eating this.

Carla looked up as he entered the dining room and met his puzzled stare. As usual, she had set a place for him at the table he preferred, yet he had been late, or absent from meals, so often that she was surprised to see him here at only a few minutes after seven.

'Aren't you rather early with dinner tonight?' he asked after responding to the greetings of the elderly paying guests.

'I didn't think you would mind if we ate early tonight, Doctor Ross. You see Robin Muir has promised to come at eight o'clock to provide some music, so I — '

'Whose idea was that?' David Ross's mouth was tight as he asked the question.

'It was Robin's idea.' Carla began to feel uncomfortable. To see that she ought not, perhaps, to have accepted Robin's offer without first consulting Dr Ross.

'Yes, I'm sure it was.'

'He thought, and I agreed, that it might cheer everyone up as they've been getting so depressed and anxious since Mrs Ross went into hospital. Perhaps you hadn't noticed, with being so busy,' she added, unwisely as it happened.

'Of course, I've noticed! It's part of my job to notice things like that,' he told her sharply. 'I just haven't had the opportunity to do anything about it yet.'

'I'll get your meal, Doctor,' she said hurriedly. 'We would have waited, of course, if we had known that you would be in to dinner tonight.'

With that, she hurried to the kitchen to hot up the individual steak pie she had made for the doctor. When she placed it before him he spoke to her again. 'I suppose you've been feeling a bit low yourself, having no young company here, and no time off since you came?'

She flushed as she answered him. 'That wasn't why I wanted Robin Muir to come tonight.'

'I didn't say it was, but it could be one reason why he's so eager to come here again, I suppose.'

Carla frowned. 'I don't follow you, Doctor.'

'Don't you? Then you must be extraordinarily naïve my dear, and I don't think you are.'

Carla bit her lip. She had heard enough. Dr Ross seemed under the impression that she had deliberately encouraged Robin Muir to come here because she wanted his company, but he was wrong about that. It was no time to argue with him though, when the residents who had not yet been served with their fruit were becoming impatient. She was here to do a job, and she would get on with it and try not to mind about the disapproval Dr Ross had shown because Robin Muir was coming here this evening. Plainly, he had something against Robin. Or maybe he was just at odds with himself and everyone around him tonight after yet another exhausting day, she decided as she moved amongst the small tables with the dishes of fruit and cream.

By a quarter to eight the dining room was empty and set up for breakfast the next day, while the spacious lounge next door to it was lit by a glowing fire around which gathered most of the residents eagerly awaiting the arrival of Robin. When he came she would bring him in and introduce him to the few who had not already met him, then make her escape. That should be easy enough to do, because if Dr Ross was going out again, as he so often did, she would have his dog to walk. That should keep her out of Robin's way at least for some of the time. Even as the thought came into her mind, the front door bell began to ring.

'Hello, Carla,' Robin greeted her as she opened the door to him.

'Hello!' Her voice echoed her astonishment at the sight of him because Robin, already a good looking young man, looked brilliant in a lounge suit of excellent cut and finest dove grey cloth, a dazzling white silk shirt and a tie of colourful silk. He looked so different from the man she saw every day wearing grubby cords and a shabby pullover that she was lost for words. It took her a couple of moments to register the fact that behind him, carrying a Spanish guitar, was his sister.

'Morag thought she'd come along and help out as well,' Robin said by way of explanation. Yet he did not look altogether pleased because she was there.

'I'm glad you came Morag,' Carla told her warmly, and thought how stunningly attractive Robin's sister looked in her low necked frilled white blouse and swirling rainbow printed skirt.

When the brother and sister were installed in the lounge and surrounded by the inhabitants of the manor, Carla begged them to excuse her so that she could exercise Dr Ross's dog for him.

Morag, it seemed, was disappointed to hear that. 'Isn't David here? I was certain I'd seen his car when we arrived.'

'He's here, but he probably had to go out again. So I'll have to walk his dog,' Carla explained.

'You'll come and join us later, though?' That was Robin's voice breaking in when she had thought that all his attention was on the piano keyboard.

'Yes. I'll be bringing in some coffee for you later.'

'And helping us to sing, I hope?' he persisted.

'If I have time,' she replied evasively without meeting his eyes.

Then she was out in the hall again, and half regretting that she had been so offhand with Robin, because seen against this new setting and in his unfamiliar gear he looked quite devastating, and it might just have been fun to throw aside the fatigue that always descended on her at this time of the day and join in with the entertainment that she could now hear on the other side of the lounge door. Robin was an accomplished pianist and his voice blended harmoniously with that of his sister as the first verse of a well-known Scottish ballad rose into the air. The melody followed Carla as she made her way through the back hall and from there to the conservatory where Figaro spent much of his time. She could still hear it faintly when she reached the glass door behind which Dr Ross's dog would be waiting for her.

She was surprised, in the act of opening the door, to see that David Ross was already in the conservatory, and that the big black dog was standing with its forepaws on his chest while he stroked the woolly black head. Figaro did not seem to know, or care, that she was near. All his attention was on his beloved master. David Ross spoke softly to him.

'Yes, I've missed you, too, old boy.'

Carla was about to turn away, feeling unwanted, when Figaro saw her and came to give her the sort of boisterous welcome that she was now so well used to that she did not stagger back from it as she would have done a few days ago.

'What are you doing here, I thought you would have been with the music makers?' the doctor asked as she gave Figaro an affectionate caress.

'I came to give Figaro his walk, as I always do at this time.'

'It's raining tonight,' he pointed out.

'It's rained on some of the other evenings,' she reminded him. 'Figaro never seems to mind what the weather is like.'

'I was thinking about you. Perhaps I should tell you how grateful I am to you for taking over the dog walking while I've been so busy. It isn't really part of the cook's job, and Figaro can be a handful.'

'I don't mind.'

'I suppose I ought to have put him into kennels, the way things are at present. I can still do that, if you are finding it a bit too much for you.'

'Oh, but he'd fret, wouldn't he? He'd think he was being abandoned again. He won't have forgotten yet, will he?' As Carla spoke, Figaro licked her hand.

'No. Maybe he'll never forget. It isn't the sort of thing one can easily leave behind, being rejected by those we love and trusted. Those we thought also loved us. Those we thought were our whole world.' David Ross's face was bleak as he spoke.

Carla felt her throat swell as she listened to him. But there was so little, if anything, that she could do to ease the anguish for him. It was different for Figaro, a walk in the rain, a chase after a stick, a kind word from his master and his world was again full of joy. For David Ross the only solace must be in doing his job.

'I don't mind taking Figaro out,' she said quickly, to cover her emotion. 'I'm used to him now, and I enjoy the fresh air after being shut in the kitchen with the cooker going full blast. You ought to rest, Doctor Ross. You look so tired,' she added.

'I am tired,' he admitted. 'Too tired to sleep some nights. Perhaps some fresh air would help me, as I'm not on call tonight. Shall we both go with him, if you are not in a hurry to join the singers? I could put you in the picture about how things are with Mother while we are walking.'

'Yes.'

Carla was already zipping up her anorak while the doctor clipped the lead on to his dog. He held open the door that led into the garden and waited for her to precede him.

'It's stopped raining now,' he said.

Instinctively, Carla took the footpath that lay in the opposite direction from the ford. She had noticed that Figaro had a tendency to make for the ford, and the Ford House, when he was with her as though hoping always to find his absent master there, but she would not let him take that route ever. She had not forgotten yet how furious Dr Ross had been when he discovered her and the dog at his home and accused her of trespassing.

'If we go into the wood we can let Figaro off the lead for a while as there are no animals grazing there,' David Ross suggested. 'I'm never too sure of how Figaro will behave if there are sheep about and I don't want to take any risks with him and find myself at odds with the farmer.'

'That's what I was afraid of the other day, when he pulled away from me and ran down to the ford,' Carla broke in. 'I could see the sheep on the hill and I was so frightened that he would chase them — '

'Instead of which, he made for his old home and I came chasing down to give you a ticking off,' David finished for her. 'I'm sorry I lost my temper with you as I did. Unfortunately I'm rather unpredictable just now. Afterwards, I wondered if you would decide I was too ill tempered and walk out on me, but you didn't, thank God.'

They were into the wood now, walking slowly because of the gnarled branches beneath their feet, while Figaro chased a rabbit. Carla felt the tension slipping away from her, leaving her calm and at peace with herself and David Ross.

'I knew you were under some stress, with your mother so ill and all the responsibility for her business being thrust on to you,' she said quietly.

He sighed. 'That's not the whole of it, either. There are other problems, but you were not exactly without problems yourself when you came here, were you? I remember having the feeling that you were running away from something, some situation which you could no longer endure. Are things any easier for you now?'

'Yes,' she answered thoughtfully. 'I think they are. Maybe because up here I'm far enough removed from the people who hurt me so much. Though I do worry about how my father will manage when my sister gets married.'

'Was that what you were running away from, your sister's marriage?'

'Yes.'

'Do you want to talk about it?'

'There's not much to tell. Just that Jane is going to marry the man I had thought was in love with me.'

'That must have made things very difficult for you?'

'Yes. Worse than that. I tried hard to get used to the idea, but when my sister started talking about the wedding over every meal I just couldn't take any more. So I decided to come up to Yorkshire and look for a job.'

'And found yourself dragged into our kitchen before you had time to catch your breath,' he said in an amused voice. 'You must have thought I'd taken leave of my senses, at first, but how glad I am that you decided to stay with us.'

Carla laughed. 'So am I, now!'

'Are you really? I feel guilty about the way we've had to take advantage of your good nature, whenever I have time to think about it,' he told her ruefully.

'It wasn't really my good nature,' she admitted then. 'I just didn't know what else to do with myself, once I got here. How to fill my life, without Emile.'

'You must have loved him very much?'

'He was the first man I'd ever cared deeply for, apart from my father. He came into my life just after my mother died, at a time when I was feeling so low, and so lonely, and he gave me something to look forward to again. That is, until he met Jane when she came back to England after breaking her engagement to the man she was planning to marry in Canada. I suppose I'll have to go back home one day, but I don't know how I'll bear it because Emile and Jane will be living fairly close to our bookshop, above the restaurant Emile manages for his parents.'

'You'll cope, when the time comes, because you are really quite a strong person, Carla. Did you know that?'

She stopped, and turned to face him, trying to

read his face in the gathering gloom. 'Do you think so? When I ran away from my home and my job as I did?'

'I think you've grown up since then. Matured, and learned how to deal with difficult situations, as you have managed to do in my household. One day you'll learn to love again, and to be happy again.'

'Will I?'

He touched her cheek with a gentle finger, trying to smooth away the sadness from around her mouth. 'Yes, I'm certain you will.'

Abruptly then he dropped his fingers as he spoke, almost to himself.

'I wish I could be as sure of — '

'Of what, Doctor?' she murmured.

He sighed. 'The name is David, and the only thing I'm sure of right now is that it's going to rain again. So we'd better run for home.'

Calling to his dog, he took Carla's hand and hurried her through the wood. Overhead, a blackbird filled the air with the sweetness of his song.

There was, for Carla, a hint of mockery in that sweet melody and in the words David Ross had just said to her. How could she ever be as happy again, without Emile?

Yet it was comforting to feel her hand firmly enclosed in David's as they raced homewards through the rain, with Figaro leading the way.

Six

By the time Carla and David reached the house they were quite wet, yet her damp clothes and straggly hair were soon forgotten because all about her now was the sound of lively music as Robin Muir beat out the cheerful melody on the piano, and the voices of the retired show business folk joined enthusiastically in singing the words.

'Are you going to join them, Carla?' David asked as she shook the moisture from her hair.

'Are you, Doctor?'

'David,' he corrected her. 'No, Carla. It isn't my kind of thing. I prefer serious music, but I thought I'd have an early night, while I get the chance.'

'Shall I make you some coffee before I take theirs into the lounge?'

'Yes, please, but I'll have it in here. If I go into my office and sit down with the newspaper I'll probably fall asleep over it,' he told her with a smile.

He watched from his seat at the kitchen table as she set out cups and saucers and filled china dishes with some of the fancy biscuits she had made earlier in the day. Her movements were quick and neat. She was very much at home in this large, well appointed room now.

'Life should be a bit easier for you from next week,' he told her. 'Because Mrs Golightly will be well enough to come back to work then. You'll find her a tower of strength. She doesn't get involved with the cooking, but she's an expert at house-keeping and also very good with the old dears.'

Carla paused in the act of filling a cream jug. 'I'm afraid I've never been able to catch up with all the dusting and polishing.'

'I'm not surprised. You've had your work cut out keeping us all well fed. That's all I expected of you, Carla.'

'Will Mrs Ross be coming home soon?'

She caught his startled look, and was puzzled for a moment. Too late, she realised that he had misunderstood her.

'I meant — your mother, David.'

His features relaxed then. 'I don't want her to come straight back here when she's fit to leave hospital. I'd like her to go somewhere warm for a while, but she isn't keen on the idea. She seems to think this place will fall apart without her and is determined to get back to it as soon as she is fit. Or even before she's fit.'

Carla placed the coffee pot on the hob to keep hot. In that moment an idea came into her head. Impulsively she spoke of it.

'Would it help if I were to go and see your mother at the hospital one day, David? I might be able to reassure her that I can manage to keep things going until she is well again.'

His face lit with eagerness. 'Would you do that for me?'

'Yes, of course.'

'I'm sure it will help.'

'I'll go as soon as Mrs Golightly is back, so that she will be here to keep an eye on things while I'm out. Now I'd better take the coffee in, while they are having a rest from the singing,' she told him.

Her appearance with the coffee and biscuits was greeted by a round of applause from the elderly residents, who all seemed to be in good humour, but there was a look of reproach in Robin Muir's eyes as she handed him a cup and saucer.

'What happened to you, Carla? I thought you were never coming. The evening is nearly over,' he complained.

'I told you, I had to walk Doctor Ross's dog – '

'Even when he is here to do it himself?'

'Yes. I needed some fresh air.'

As she spoke, Carla was aware of Morag watching them intently and listening to their exchange of words.

'Isn't David joining us for coffee?' Morag asked. 'He always used to.'

'He's very tired, so he's having an early night. Things have been very hectic for him during this last couple of weeks, he's been called out so many times at night, with the practice being short of one doctor,' Carla tried to explain.

'He's lucky to have had you to help him, with the dog and everything. After all, that can't be part of the cook's job,' Robin commented.

'I'd have helped him, if he'd asked,' Morag sounded put out. 'Only he didn't.'

'I expect he thought you had enough to do at the market garden. You always seem to be busy there,

I don't suppose Robin can do without you,' Carla told her.

'All the same, he could have asked — '

'It'll be easier for us next week, because Mrs Golightly is coming back,' Carla broke in, seeing Robin frowning at his sister.

'You'll have more time to yourself then, Carla, won't you?' All the darkness was gone from Robin's face as he voiced that thought.

Carla hesitated. 'I don't know. I'm not sure yet how things will work out. How late Mrs Golightly will be able to work.'

'It's more than time you had an evening off. Surely Ross can't expect you to be here every evening as well as every day?' Robin said sharply.

'I've nothing else to do with my time. No friends or relatives up here,' she began, then knew it to be a mistake.

'You have me, Carla. You must know that I've been waiting for you to have a free evening so I can take you out. I've mentioned it before. Aren't you longing to get away from here for a while? To spend your time with someone nearer your own age? To have a meal cooked for you by someone else? I promise I'll give you a good time, Carla. So when shall it be?'

How could she snub him when his dark eyes were kindling with such warmth, when admiration was written all over his handsome face? His obvious attraction to her was a great boost to her morale. The feeling of rejection which had been haunting her, day and night, ever since Emile confessed to being in love with her sister diminished in that moment. Here was a personable

man begging for her company. She need no longer
feel alone and unwanted. Robin Muir was promis-
ing to banish those feelings, and she heard herself
accepting him.

'Later in the week, perhaps.'

'How about Wednesday?' Robin suggested.
'There's a folk music night at the Miller's Inn on
Wednesdays and they do very good bar suppers
there. Shall I collect you about eight?'

Only when she had agreed to that did Robin
return to the piano, this time to sing as well as play
a Burns' love song. As he sang his gaze lingered all
the time on Carla. It was a moving experience for
her, even though she had no way of knowing
whether or not he was sincere. Even if he was, she
would find it hard to believe him. She would not
allow herself to be hurt again by him or any man.
Yet she could appreciate why Bessie and most of
the other old ladies adored him because when the
singing was over and he went round the room
shaking hands with them, sometimes kissing the
hand of one of the prettier elderly women, like
Miss Clare, he made them feel young again and
desirable again. With his going the atmosphere of
the room lost much of its warmth and excitement.

During the next couple of days Carla found
herself wondering if she had been wise to accept
Robin's invitation because on her visits to the
market garden there was now a subtle change in
his attitude towards her. Nothing she was able to
define exactly, maybe it was merely in her imagination. Yet she did not think so and was
vaguely uneasy.

On the Monday morning she met Mrs Golightly

for the first time and took an immediate liking to her, perhaps because she reminded her so strongly of her own mother. Mrs Golightly was brisk, cheerful and kind, a woman who got things done with a minimum of fuss. It would be easy to leave the manor and its inhabitants in her care while she took some time off at last, so Carla accepted Dr Ross's offer to drive to the cottage hospital with him to visit his mother.

The splendour of autumn colourings was all about them as they drove the ten miles to the small cathedral city where the hospital was situated. David Ross appeared much more relaxed today than he had been recently as he pointed out a few places of interest to Carla. Some of these she recalled from her childhood holidays, others she planned to visit when she had the time.

'It's a glorious area to live in,' he told her when she admired one wide and wonderful vista of broad river and bracken clad hills. 'As long as you are not hankering after city people and city ways,' he added, almost to himself.

'Yes,' she agreed. 'When we used to come here my parents always said they would come to live here when they sold the business and retired. I don't know how Dad feels about it now that he's on his own.'

'It isn't so long since your mother died, I take it?'

'A couple of years.'

'So they'd been married a long time, like my parents?'

'Yes.'

'They were the lucky ones.'

Carla turned her head to stare at him with a

puzzled frown. 'The lucky ones? To be left alone — '

'To have had so many long and happy years together, was what I meant,' he told her quietly.

They were entering the hospital car park now, so there was no need for her to try and follow that remark. Yet the remark stayed in her mind as she walked with David along the corridor until they came to the private room which was occupied by his mother. There he introduced Carla, who handed over the chrysanthemums she had bought from the market garden, then said he had another patient to visit in the men's ward and would come back later.

'You are much younger than I expected,' Mrs Ross told Carla after thanking her for the flowers. 'I've been asking David about you ever since I began to feel better, but he's been quite evasive. So I hardly know anything about you.'

'That's probably because he hasn't had the time to get to know me. He's been out of the house so much, with having extra work to do in the practice, and if he has been in he's been terribly tired,' Carla tried to explain.

'It must have been very hard for you, taking over at such a time with me in here and Mrs Golightly ill as well. Even Mrs Golightly's daughter hasn't been able to help you as she would have done because her children have been so ill. I don't know how you've managed,' the older woman said.

'I've had Bessie to help me, and I just concentrated on the cooking and the shopping while Bessie did what she could to keep the rooms tidy.'

Mrs Ross gave her a rueful smile. 'Bessie can be

a mixed blessing. If she likes you, she's marvellous. If she doesn't, you are in trouble. We lost our last cook at rather short notice, and at the worst possible time, because Bessie did not like her enough to work harmoniously with her.'

'She can be rather bossy, but she seems to like me; to have accepted me.'

'Perhaps that's because you know how to handle her tactfully?' Mrs Ross suggested. 'Yet I would have thought you rather young to have learned how to do that. How long is it since you left catering college, my dear?'

Carla began to feel uncomfortable. Plainly, David had not told his mother the truth about her arrival at Ravensford Manor, and how he had bundled her into the kitchen there on the assumption that she was a new cook from the agency when she had only gone there looking for a room.

'Of course, we were lucky to get you at such short notice after that awful woman quarrelled like a fish wife with Bessie, then walked out when I was too ill to act as peacemaker. No wonder David was so glad to see you,' his mother continued. 'But how did you happen to be available at such short notice?' Where had you been working before you came to us?'

Carla bit her lip. It would have to be the truth for Mrs Ross, because her work documents would reveal this anyway as soon as David's mother returned home. 'I was working for my father at his bookshop in London,' she said.

'What were you doing there? Filling in time between jobs, or are you just out of college?'

'No. I left college when my mother was very ill,

so that I could look after her and Dad.'

Mrs Ross looked bewildered. 'How did you come to be in Yorkshire then, at the time we needed you? I mean, if you were working at your father's bookshop.'

'I came up here because I wanted to get away from home for a while, for personal reasons. I was planning to look for a job, but I just went to the manor in search of a room because I remembered having stayed there with my parents a number of years ago. I didn't know it was no longer a hotel, and when I rang the bell Dr Ross thought I was the woman he was expecting from the agency in Leeds. I tried to explain, but I couldn't seem to get through to him because he was in such a hurry to get out to some emergency call. He rushed me into the kitchen and left me there with Bessie, who said it was time I got on with cooking the dinner,' Carla finished wryly.

'And you did just that?' Mrs Ross's voice was full of her astonishment.

Carla shrugged her shoulders. 'What else could I do? Bessie couldn't do the heavy lifting on her own, and I knew there was some sort of crisis going on. So I stayed and helped. I had nothing else to do with my time,' she added.

Mrs Ross began to laugh until her merriment filled the room. Only when she had managed to get her breath back did she speak. 'I'd love to have seen my son's face when he discovered the truth. What did he say?'

'He didn't know until a few hours later, when he was back from the emergency call and had eaten the dinner I'd cooked. The woman he had been expecting telephoned then and told him she had got her car stuck in the ford and been forced to go back to Leeds to change her wet clothes. I had to explain then that all I'd wanted was a room,' Carla smiled at the recollection. 'I don't think he could quite believe that it was really all his fault, at first. When he did, he offered me the job.'

'And you took it. I wonder why? It must be so different from what you've been used to — '

'Perhaps I wanted to do something different, and I had been used to cooking for my father and my sister and sometimes for guests. Adapting to the much larger number was just common sense, really. And there was Bessie to help.'

'Will you be staying on?'

'I hope so.'

'Don't you find it lonely, with no other young people around you?'

Carla laughed. 'I haven't had time to be lonely, Mrs Ross. By the time I've cooked dinner and taken Figaro out if Dr Ross is working, which he usually is, it's time to serve late night drinks and go to bed.'

'It doesn't sound as if you've had much time off so far.'

'I don't mind. It isn't as if I had any family or friends up here.'

'All the same, you can't go on like that. I shall come home tomorrow and see that you do get some off duty time,' Mrs Ross said firmly.

'Oh, but David said — ' Carla broke off.

'What did David say?'

'That you might be going away for a few weeks to somewhere warm and sunny to convalesce.'

'Did he? I shall make my own decision about that, when I'm back home in a day or two,' Mrs Ross told her, and Carla knew that David was going to have a new problem to solve.

'Please don't come home for my sake, Mrs Ross. I really can cope,' she hastened to assure the dainty little lady who was proving to be so determined. Yet when she left her a few minutes later and was walking back to his car with David she knew that Mrs Ross was not convinced that they could go on managing at Ravensford Manor without her. She mentioned this to David when he opened the door for her to slip into the passenger seat beside him.

'I intend to be very firm with her. She really isn't fit to do as much as she used to do,' David said with a frown.

'She seems to be worrying because I haven't had any time off. I couldn't convince her that it hasn't worried me.'

'You'll have more time off, from now on, Carla. Starting with this afternoon. I've arranged for Mrs Golightly to serve the teas, so there's no reason why we shouldn't have tea here before we go back. Would you like to do that? Or have you other plans?'

Carla was too surprised at first to reply. Then she saw doubt creep into his face.

'Yes, I'd like to have tea here,' she hastened to assure him.

His face cleared then. 'Good. Let's go.'

He did not speak to her again until the hospital had been left behind and they were driving towards the market place. It was evident that he knew his way about the bustling streets because soon they were parked behind a bow-windowed teashop.

'I think you'll like it here. It's the best place for miles around,' he told her as he steered her past a display of home-made chocolates to where a number of small tables were situated. 'Though it's a long time since I was last here,' he added.

Yet in spite of that the elderly waitress who came to take their order remembered him. 'It's nice to see you here again, Doctor Ross. We've missed you, and Mrs Ross.'

She beamed at Carla and did not seem to be aware of her mistake.

Carla felt hot colour flood her cheeks as she waited for David to correct the woman. He made no attempt to do so. Instead he glanced down the menu, then placed an order for hot scones and cream cakes to accompany the pot of tea.

'I'm sorry, David,' Carla mumbled, since it seemed to her that he must be hurt by the reference to his missing wife.

'Why? It isn't your fault that the waitress took you for Giselle, or even hers, as there is a similarity in age, height and colouring between you, and it must be over a year since I brought Giselle here.'

Further discussion was halted by the return of the waitress with their tea. After Carla had poured this they turned to a different topic, begun by Carla.

'I had to tell your mother the truth about how I came to be cooking at the manor. I hope you don't mind, but I thought that if she did come home tomorrow, as she's threatening to do, and saw my work documents, she would be asking some questions anyway.'

'Did you tell her it all? About the way I dragged you in and thrust you into the kitchen when all you wanted was a bedroom for the night?' His lips twitched as he asked that.

'Yes. She thought it was very funny.'

'I don't suppose you were quite so amused at the time, Carla,' he said as he saw her smile.

She looked down at her plate. 'I think I was feeling too miserable to care much what happened to me,' she said in a low voice.

'And now?'

His eyes were resting on her face, but she could not lift her own gaze to meet them. He was perceptive enough to be able to read her thoughts, perhaps, and she did not want him to guess that all her sympathy was for him now and not for herself.

'I've learned to live with it. To accept what happened to me,' she murmured.

His hand reached out to touch hers for a moment. 'One has to do that,' he told her. 'It has to be taken in perspective. Faced up to, then set aside so that we can get on with our lives. In my work I see so many tragedies. Most of them make what happened to us, to you and to me, seem quite trivial by comparison. At least we are here, young and with our health. We can choose whether to wallow in self-pity for ever, or to pick up the pieces and begin again. Don't you agree?'

'Yes,' she answered, without hesitation.

'You are ready then, to begin again?'

Her answer seemed to be of vital importance to him, something in the way he waited for it warned her. In the moment that she acknowledged that, she felt for the first time in months a lifting of her spirits. A small, almost imperceptible, surge of happiness.

'Yes, I think I am,' she said breathlessly.

He laughed softly. 'Then you'd better start by sampling one of those cream cakes. Later, we'll talk about what to do with your off-duty hours. I have a few ideas about that.'

His ideas, she discovered as they enjoyed the food and emptied the teapot, were for exploration of the district by car and on foot. Even for an excursion into the nearby Lake District to see the autumn foliage at Tarn Howes. She was a little puzzled by the way he used the term 'we' so often in talking of these outings. Was he, perhaps, planning to share them with her? The idea made her heart beat faster. She found herself liking him more than ever now that they were away from the place where both were always so busy. All too soon the shared tea was finished and it was time to leave for Ravensford.

'I must take some of those chocolates for my mother,' he told her as they were making their way out of the teashop. 'They are her favourites.'

So, while he went to the counter to choose and pay for his purchases, she went to stare at the selection of dark, rich, confectionery for which this firm was renowned. There were chocolates topped with walnuts, with cherries, with almonds, chocolates filled with cream and brandy or rum truffle. Was David hoping to soften up his mother with this gift, to persuade her not to return yet to Ravensford Manor? She saw him stop to speak to someone who was also buying a box of chocolates, but only for a moment. He was frowning when he rejoined her.

'Do you think the chocolates will help?' she asked as they walked to his car.

'Help?' He looked at her blankly.

'To change Mrs Ross's mind about going away for a while.'

He grinned at her. 'It will take more than that to change Mother's mind, she's a very determined woman,' he said as he tossed the carrier bag containing the sweets on to the back seat.

The drive back to Ravensford through the sunlit dale was over too soon and they were coming to a halt in the courtyard behind the house, with the thought in both their minds that their brief spell of freedom was over and they were back to the place that held work and responsibility for them. It was time for Carla to express her thanks.

'I've enjoyed it so much. Thank you, David.'

'So have I. More than I've enjoyed anything for ages. We must do it again, before long.'

As he reached across to open the door for her Carla felt again a fleeting moment of happiness. Fleeting, but disturbing.

'I'd better go and get dinner started,' she said hurriedly.

'Wait, Carla.'

She turned back and saw that he was holding out a gift wrapped package he had taken from the carrier bag.

'For me?' Her eyes widened.

'A token of thanks, from Figaro and me, for the walks and everything,' he said awkwardly, as if he did not often give presents.

Carla felt quite ridiculously happy then, but all she could say was a hasty, 'Thank you, David.'

Then, clutching the chocolates, she ran to her room to change into one of the cool blouses and cotton skirts she always wore in the kitchen.

The feeling of happiness persisted, so that she found herself singing along with Bessie as they cooked the dinner that evening. It was because she had been away from the manor for a while and come back refreshed, she told herself, not because she had spent an hour alone with David Ross and he had talked of them sharing other outings. She would feel the same when she had spent an evening with Robin Muir. It was a sign that she was recovering at last from her long weeks of loneliness and despair.

Seven

The evening spent with Robin Muir did not, though, have the same effect on Carla as her brief hour or two with David had done. In fact, it all went out of gear right from the start when Bessie got involved in an argument with Mrs Golightly over who should carry up a tray with light food to old Joe, who was the latest victim of the 'flu virus.

'I'll do it, like I've always done if anyone is ill,' Mrs Golightly told Bessie firmly. 'The trays are too heavy for you, Bessie.'

'I managed well enough while you were away, and Joe is my special friend, so I want to look after him,' Bessie retorted.

'There's no need, now I'm back,' Mrs Golightly insisted.

'Joe would rather see me, I know he would.'

'He won't care who he sees as long as he gets his food.'

'Haven't you enough to do in the kitchen, helping Carla? She's going out tonight, so she won't want to be late with the meal.'

Bessie's glowering face told Carla that it was time to intervene. In this mood, Bessie could not be reasoned with.

'I'll take the tray, I'm going up anyway to wash my hair.' Mrs Golightly smiled at her, but Bessie scowled and stamped off to bang the kitchen door as hard as she could. Her black mood persisted until Carla could have blown her top at the way she would not be hurried, and would not accept help with any of her usual duties. Not even with the preparation of the very small Brussels sprouts which Carla knew she detested doing.

'You'll make us very late, Bessie, if you don't move over and let me help,' Carla said, keeping her own temper with an effort.

'Won't hurt them to wait, for once,' Bessie said morosely.

Carla tightened her lips. 'But Doctor Ross will be kept waiting too. He said he would be in to dinner tonight.'

'He won't mind waiting,' Bessie grunted. 'He won't have to!'

Carla took a deep breath. 'I don't intend to be late, Bessie, because I'm going out, for once,' she declared. 'So please get a move on.'

They were late though, so that Robin was at the door to collect Carla before the meal was finished. 'Sorry I'm not ready, Robin,' Carla told him. 'I'll just finish serving the pudding, then I'll leave Bessie to clear away.'

Robin grinned. 'I can wait. I won't go without you,' he said.

Ought she to show him into the lounge, Carla wondered. If she did so he would soon become involved in talking to some of the old dears, and then they would be later than ever in getting to the Miller's Inn. It was Robin who made the decision for her.

'I'll wait here for you,' he said, lowering his tall frame on to one of the kitchen chairs. 'I won't get in the way, I promise.'

A moment later, Bessie came stamping in from the dining room. Her face filled with delight when she saw Robin. Then she turned accusingly on Carla. 'You didn't tell us he was coming to play for us tonight. We could have hurried up and had everything cleared away by now.'

Carla held on to her temper with an effort. She felt tired, hot, and very harassed. Before she could say anything Robin had the situation in hand.

'Carla didn't tell you because I haven't come to play the piano tonight, Bessie. I've come to take Carla out for a couple of hours. Don't you think she deserves to go out, after working so hard these last weeks?'

Bessie scowled at him. 'She could have had a night off and joined in with the singing. It's miserable here without Mrs Ross. We thought she was ready to come home, and now she's had a relapse.'

'I'll come another night, Bessie. Perhaps later in the week,' he tried to pacify her.

Bessie became belligerent. 'You won't! You'll forget, like you managed to forget about us right from last winter.'

'That's enough Bessie! Go and finish your dinner at once!'

David Ross spoke sharply from the open door that led into the dining room. His glance left Bessie then and moved to Carla.

'You'd better go, Carla. We can manage without

you now.' His eyes moved on to Robin Muir, cool, appraising, and the next words were addressed to him.

'You won't want to waste your time here, will you?'

'I can wait,' Robin said calmly.

David took the coffee pot from Carla. 'As I said, we can manage. You'd better go, Carla.'

He was dismissing her as he would have sent away his dog when he was displeased with it, Carla thought as she recognised the anger in his eyes even though his voice was calm and controlled. She found herself shivering as she went up the stairs at speed to change her clothes and wash her face.

Later, as she and Robin drove towards the Miller's Inn, Robin Muir gave her his opinion. 'He wasn't pleased because you were coming out with me, was he?'

'I thought he seemed glad to get rid of me,' she joked. 'He was only saying a couple of days ago that I ought to get out more.'

'Perhaps it was me he wanted to get rid of. In fact, I'm sure.'

Carla laughed. 'Why? Have you got a bad reputation, Robin?'

There was no answering smile from Robin. 'I guess as far as he's concerned I have.'

'Do you deserve it?' she asked, sobering suddenly.

'That isn't for me to say. He seems to have made his mind up.'

These enigmatic remarks intrigued Carla, but there was no time for her to find out what lay behind them because Robin was steering his car into the car park behind the Miller's Inn, and already she could hear the strains of folk song which told her the ceilidh had already begun.

Once inside the inn it was easy enough for her to forget all about her trying day at Ravensford Manor and the coldness with which David Ross had despatched her for the evening out he had so strongly urged her to take. It was only later, when she was driving away from the inn with Robin that it all came back to her, and with it a feeling of unease.

'Are you coming back to our place for a coffee?' Robin asked as they neared Ravensford.

She hesitated. 'It's nearly midnight, Robin, and I have to be up early in the morning.'

'So have I, but a coffee won't take long to drink. You haven't seen our place yet, have you? Only the market garden and the farm shop. The house is rather nice.'

Still she was reluctant. 'It's been a long day — '

He laughed. 'You sound just like one of your old dears, Carla. Be your age, be daring and stay out of your prison for as long as you can. I told Morag you would probably come back with me.'

'It isn't a prison to me. I like it there,' she insisted.

'But you must be glad to get away from it sometimes — '

She smiled. 'I was tonight, with Bessie in such a foul mood.'

'So make a night of it. Live dangerously and have coffee with me.'

It seemed then that she must have agreed because he drove past the entrance to the manor and on to the substantial stone built house behind which was his market garden. There were lights on in the house, making it appear welcoming, so Carla stifled her doubts and allowed him to lead her into his home. The room into which he took her was well, but plainly, furnished with a deep leather sofa and matching chairs. There were bookshelves flanking the stone fireplace and these held a few foliage plants, but there were no flowers and no cushions. Nothing to be seen of a woman's touch. It was very much a man's room. So where was the influence of Morag, surely to be expected if she shared her brother's home? As she waited for Robin to reappear with the coffee she could not banish this thought from her mind.

'Coffee for my lady,' Robin said lightly as he came into the room with a couple of china beakers. 'My reluctant lady.'

He looked suddenly too large, too handsome, too male as he set the beakers on a low table near the sofa where she was sitting. She knew herself to be too vulnerable.

'Where's Morag?' she asked. 'I thought you said she was expecting to see me?'

'She's probably gone to bed. She doesn't wait up for me, darling, even if we do share this house. In fact, we each have our own separate apartments. This is mine, hers is upstairs.' He dropped his long frame on to the sofa beside Carla as he finished speaking.

'But I thought — '

She ought to have foreseen this, Carla knew then. She had been too trusting, too naïve. Yet she

could not reveal her uneasiness or he would laugh
at her. All she could do was to drink her coffee
quickly, then make her escape.

'You didn't really think Morag would be here?
That I'd be willing to share you with her? I've had
you to myself so seldom since I met you, Carla,
that you mustn't grudge me an hour or so of your
time tonight. I won't keep you too late, I promise,
darling.'

Carla sighed. Robin could be so disarming, so
utterly charming. Yet when she set down her mug
of coffee because it was too hot to drink he lost no
time in drawing her firmly into his arms and
holding her so close that she could feel the heat
and the desire in him. She felt trapped.

'Relax, darling,' he urged as she tensed her body
into resistance. 'You are away from your old
ladies, and your cold fish of a doctor now. You are
on your own, and you are young and beautiful,
and I'm falling more and more in love with you.'

His kiss was too long, too intense, too intimate.
At first she found herself submitting to it, giving
way to her own loneliness and longing. Yet as one
kiss became another and the caresses became ever
more urgent and demanding she felt an instinctive
withdrawal from him, the knowledge that however handsome and charming Robin might be he
was not irresistible to her. Maybe it was too soon
for her to fall in love again. Maybe she would
never want that sort of love again. Certainly she
did not want to share it with this man. Sureness of
that helped her to wriggle out of his embrace and
somehow get to her feet.

'I'll have to go, Robin,' the words came tumbling

out too hurriedly.

'What's the hurry? You haven't even drunk your coffee. He won't be waiting up for you, your cold fish doctor, will he?'

The words struck a chord in Carla's mind, reminded her of what she ought to have done before coming out.

'He might *have* to wait up for me, because I have no key to the house. I've never needed one because I haven't been out late in the evening before. So I *will* have to go, Robin.'

He gave a sigh of exasperation. 'Just my luck. Or bad luck!' He rose to his feet with a comical look of resignation on his face. 'Do bring your key next time, Carla my sweet.'

Carla did not answer. She was too busy buttoning her jacket, smoothing down her skirt, picking up her shoulder bag, and all the time longing to be back at the manor. To be safe with her old dears, and her cold fish of a doctor, as Robin had called him. Safe from this man who wanted her to fall in love again too soon, when she was not yet ready to do that.

She was silent on the short drive to the manor, and Robin did not have much to say, but as they speeded up the long curving drive he pointed to the light that shone out from the front of the house.

'He's waiting up for you.'

'At least I won't have to knock him up so that I can get in. It was stupid of me not to think about bringing a key. Thanks for taking me to the folk night, Robin. I really enjoyed it,' she added as he stopped the car.

'All of it?' he asked. 'I hoped you would.' He caught her mouth again in a long, hard kiss that she found distasteful, then allowed her to go with a hurried 'goodnight'.

Carla stumbled up the front steps and into the silent house. A thin line of light showed from under the door of the office. As she dropped the latch on the front door, Carla looked towards it and wondered whether David had heard her come in. She crept to the office door and listened. No sound came from within. Ought she to let him know that she was back? It was difficult for her to decide. If he *had* heard her he would surely have come out of his office to say goodnight, or just to make certain the door was now locked. She tapped gently on the nearest panel and opened the door sufficiently to be able to peep inside, just enough for her to be able to see the figure sprawled in the high-backed chair before the desk. David had fallen asleep while reading a medical journal.

Carla's fingers tightened on the doorframe as she let her eyes dwell on his relaxed features, his tousled rusty brown hair, his strongly marked brows, his freckled complexion and square jaw-line. It came to rest on his mouth, full and firm-lipped. She was unable to drag her gaze away from David's mouth. It seemed to act like a magnet to her own lips, which felt raw still from Robin Muir's unwanted kisses.

Would she have pushed David away from her if he had attempted to kiss her in that way, she found herself wondering, and knew in a second what the answer was. The knowledge shocked her deeply. She had no right to be harbouring such thoughts about David Ross, because David had a wife even if that wife had for some reason walked out on him.

What sort of woman was she, this Giselle, who could stay away from him for so long when it was plain that he needed her? It was not possible to know what she looked like, since there was no photograph of her to be seen in this room or any other at Ravensford Manor. 'A bit like you in height, age and colouring,' David had told Carla that day in the teashop when the waitress had thought she was his wife.

If she had been David's wife, she would not have left him to work himself into exhaustion for his patients, to come home to a house where there were people in plenty, but not the one person who could give love and comfort when things were going wrong. If she were married to David, she would cherish him and care for him all the days of her life, be his friend and companion as well as his lover. She would share the black moments and the disturbed nights as well as the good times, and think it all worthwhile. But she was not his wife and it was dangerous to even allow herself to think of these things. So dangerous that she must never allow them to enter her mind again in case they brought to her the kind of suffering which she knew instinctively would be far worse than anything she had known before. She must not let herself fall in love with David.

In that moment, as she recognised how near she had come to doing just that, David stirred in his chair and opened his eyes. She dropped her own gaze at once, afraid that it would reveal too much of what she was feeling.

'Carla,' His voice was soft and full of reproach. 'So you are back at last.' He dragged himself to his feet and took a step towards her, his glance sharp and perceptive, seeing everything about her from her rumpled hair and creased blouse to her badly smudged lipstick.

She read his expression, and began to embark haltingly on her apology. 'I'm sorry you had to wait up for me. It was stupid of me not to have remembered to take a key with me.' She knew she was talking too quickly in an effort to cloak her confusion.

'I suppose I should think myself lucky that you came back at all.'

There was no mistaking the bitterness that clothed his words. She drew in her breath sharply, stung by the implication. Hurt by it.

'I don't know what you mean, Doctor Ross. I'm not in the habit of − ' She broke off there because she could not bring herself to go on and say that she was not in the habit of staying out all night. Of sleeping around. That he should imagine she might be was a source first of anguish then of anger to her. 'I don't know what you are implying − or even that you have a right to imply anything just because I've been out with someone for the evening and forgotten to take a key with me,' she hit back at him.

'You'd better ask Robin Muir about that. He's in a better position to tell you than I am,' came the sharp retort.

'I shall ask Robin nothing of the sort. I've apologised for keeping you up late and that's as far as I intend to go. Goodnight, Doctor,' Carla said with all the calmness she could muster, then dashed out of the room and up the stairs.

Once in her room, she flung herself down on her bed and gave way to a fit of shivering. In the space of a few hours the life which she had thought held only the satisfaction of her work had become too full of complications, of Robin Muir's unwanted admiration and of the strong pull of attraction she felt for David Ross. Perhaps it would be as well if she did not stay on at the manor, now that she knew where her feelings were leading her? She would have to consider that possibility very seriously, but not tonight, since quite suddenly exhaustion was overwhelming her and all she longed for was sleep. Without even remembering to undress fully she tumbled under the duvet and found oblivion.

It was a shock to find, the next morning, that she had overslept and was half an hour late in going down to prepare David's breakfast. Downstairs she was dismayed to see that Bessie was still in a black mood because Robin had not stayed to play the piano last night. She did not answer Carla's 'Good morning, Bessie,' and did not sing any of her usual pre-breakfast songs. The atmosphere of disapproval hung so heavily about her that Carla switched on the radio in an attempt to lighten it.

As yet, Carla had seen nothing of David this morning and guessed that he was out walking Figaro. She was not looking forward to coming face to face with him, after the way she had lost her temper last night, but she would have to do so when she served his breakfast.

It was with a fast beating heart that she took in the plate of bacon and eggs shortly after she heard him enter the dining room. She did not look at him as she placed it before him and murmured a subdued, 'Good morning, Doctor.' She moved quickly then back to the door which led into the kitchen. Before she reached it, his voice halted her feet.

'Don't go yet, Carla. I owe you an apology. I should not have said what I did to you last night, or implied something I know could not be true. I had no right, in any case, to interfere in your life. I only ask you to believe that I had your best interests at heart. Can you do that, Carla?'

She stared at him dumbly while she sought for words with which to answer. Then the telephone began to ring, so she went gladly to answer it. The call was from the Health Centre, and resulted in David bolting down his breakfast at speed and departing immediately.

Part of her was glad that there had not been time for her to take up with him where they had left off the night before. Another part wondered whether, as she had not accepted his apology at once, he would be under the impression that she had not forgiven him yet. So the day that followed was an uneasy one as she followed her now established routine of planning the meals, shopping in the village, then coming back to cook the dinner with the help of Bessie.

It did not help that Mrs Ross was quite unwell again and not fit enough either to return to her home or go to stay with her friend who lived in Spain. By now the residents were again fearful for her future and their own.

'I don't reckon we'll ever get her back,' one of them said morosely.

Bessie broke her silence to agree with him. 'No wonder Doctor David hardly ever smiles these days,' she said, shaking her head gloomily. 'First his wife left him, and now he has to manage without his mother.'

'It's only a temporary setback, Bessie,' Carla tried to comfort her. 'Mrs Ross will be home soon, you'll see.'

'I'll believe that when I see it,' Bessie declared.

Carla sighed. It was going to be a bad day, and there seemed to be little she could do about it. Even the weather was against her, with dark skies and heavy rain persisting for most of the week, while in the house the friction between Bessie and Mrs Golightly continued. David came in for meals sometimes, sometimes missed them completely as the 'flu virus continued to cause havoc in the dale. She saw little of him, and spoke to him even less.

At the market garden, each time she went to choose fresh vegetables and fruit, Robin was putting pressure on her to go out with him again. Often enough during her visits there were other customers present, or Morag was around, but Robin always made a point of carrying her goods as far as her car during the spell of wet weather, and asking her then to spend another evening with him. So far she had evaded giving a definite answer by making excuses about Bessie not being very helpful so that she was late finishing dinner every evening and too tired to want to go anywhere. Then came an afternoon when rain clouds

Doctor David

had been pushed away be warm sunshine that
turned the chestnut trees to burning gold, and
when she decided to take Figaro with her and walk
to the Muirs' market garden. Robin, working near
the entrance, saw her approaching and gave her a
quizzical glance.

'I see you've brought your minder with you
today, Carla. How are things at the manor?'

'A bit grim,' she admitted.

'What about another music night then?' He gave
her a teasing grin. 'If I can't persuade you to come
out with me, I'll come to you. Tonight, if you like.'

Carla hesitated. She did not want to spend an
evening alone with Robin, but surely there would
be no harm in him coming to play the piano for the
old dears? It could be just what they needed to lift
them out of the depression that the bad weather
and Mrs Ross's continued absence had brought on
them. It would be very selfish of her to deny them
that pleasure just because she was anxious to
avoid Robin's company. She need not be alone
with him when he came to the manor. In fact, she
would take good care not to be. So she gave him
her answer.

'Thanks, Robin. I'm sure Bessie and the others
will be delighted to see you.'

Robin laughed at that. 'It isn't Bessie and the
others I'm wanting to please, darling. It's you I'm
really coming to see.' Without even looking round
to make sure there was no one watching, he
reached across to kiss her lips with a lingering
warmth that brought no answering passion from
her. Though it did bring a warning growl from
deep in Figaro's throat.

This brought a rueful grin from Robin. 'So he really is your minder!'

Carla laughed. 'He seems to think so.' Both the dog and his master, the thought came to her then, were eager to warn her off the handsome market gardener. Why? Jealousy, perhaps, in the case of the dog who wanted all of her attention, but what of Figaro's master? What were his motives?

'Well, keep him out of the way tonight, won't you? I'd like to be sure of my welcome.'

The arrival on the scene of Morag, who made a great fuss of Figaro, brought the verbal sparring to an end. Carla noticed that Robin made no mention of his plan to visit Ravensford Manor that evening. Of course, his sister's presence would be bound to inhibit Robin, and he could not know that Carla was determined to avoid being alone with him.

As she had guessed it would, the news that Robin was to play the piano for them that evening brought an immediate lightening of Bessie's black mood. It had the same effect on many of the other residents. Only Dr Ross received the news without comment. Carla had the impression that he would like to have said things, but was restraining himself with difficulty. She had gone to his study to tell him, since he was to be in to dinner for once, that this was to be served a few minutes earlier than usual because of the hastily arranged music night. Since he made no comment, she felt bound to add one of her own.

'Robin offered to come, when I told him how depressed everyone was because Mrs Ross was not able to come home yet. I know you don't like him, but the old dears do, and they were so dis-

Doctor David

appointed that he didn't stay to play for them the other night when he called for me.'

David frowned as he replied. 'It makes little difference to me whether he comes here or not. This is my mother's house, not mine, and since she invited him in the first place I can only presume that she still does, in spite of — ' He stopped, then went on. 'I suppose you have a right to some young company, too.'

'He isn't coming to see me,' Carla put in quickly.

David stood up, as though he had little left to say. 'I can hardly believe that.'

Carla was angry with him for making that remark. It simmered in her mind all the time as she got on with preparing the evening meal in the company of a now transformed Bessie. She found it almost as hard to endure Bessie in this ebullient mood when she became very slapdash in her work, but she repressed her irritation with an effort.

Her plan to absent herself from Robin's presence as she had done on his last visit by taking Figaro out was scotched by David, who told her when she mentioned the subject that he would do the dog walking himself, since he was not on call for once. So there was to be no escape for her, she thought with resignation as she opened the front door to Robin soon afterwards. As she had expected, he was alone, and again immaculately dressed.

'Hello, Robin,' she greeted him, and took a step backwards when he would have captured her lips. He was making a habit of doing that, and it implied a sense of possession which she was beginning to resent. 'The old dears are all looking forward to seeing you.'

'Aren't you glad to see me?' he asked, frowning.

'Of course,' she told him too quickly, then hurried him into the lounge where he was welcomed rapturously.

She watched as he exuded charm and gentle courtesy, sometimes a touch of flirtation towards the old ladies, always a listening ear for the garrulous old gentlemen. Soon he was seated at the piano and filling the room with the sound of his pleasant baritone. Carla listened with pleasure, and forgot for a time all her reservations about him.

Her doubts returned when the music was over, coffee and biscuits had all been disposed of, and almost everyone had said goodnight to Robin and gone up to bed. She was tired herself, by then, but Robin seemed in no hurry to leave. Even when Bessie, the last to go, had finally departed Robin lingered, asking if he could beg another cup of coffee.

'Of course. It won't take a moment to make.' She hurried to the kitchen and set the electric kettle to boil.

A moment later, she froze as she felt a pair of arms slide around her body, felt a pair of urgent lips nuzzling into the low neckline of her blouse. She had not even realised that Robin had followed her into the kitchen, his shoes had made no sound on the carpet tiles. How was she going to get rid of him? There were no old people about now to protect her from Robin's ardour, and he seemed to take it for granted that she would not mind what he was doing with his hands. She had to get rid of him, because she could not endure what he was doing. Her attempt to move away, out of his reach, was thwarted. Yet she did not want to raise her voice in protest because David might hear her in the nearby office. David; the thought of him gave her the idea she was seeking.

'I'll have to take David, Doctor Ross, some coffee. Otherwise he'll come in to ask if I've forgotten him,' she said in an unsteady voice.

Robin was angry. 'Are you never off duty? Can't he make his own coffee?'

She ignored that, and took another china beaker from the cupboard and put too much instant coffee and too much sugar into it with a shaky hand before topping it with boiling water and moving hastily towards the door.

When she reached the hall she saw with relief that the light was still burning in the office. She tapped on the door and pushed it open.

'I've brought you some coffee, David.' She set the over-full mug down on his desk and felt some of the contents slop over her hand. At the same time she saw the empty mug that was set beside a medical textbook he had been reading.

'I've already had some. You brought mine first, remember?'

'Of course, how stupid of me to forget.' She laughed nervously, but kept her gaze on the wet ring made by the beaker she had just set down. She picked it up and rubbed at the mark it had left on the polished surface of the desk. When this had been removed she still lingered, this time to ask David about his mother.

'She's much improved today, and leaving to

convalesce tomorrow, though I'm certain I told you that only a couple of hours ago, Carla.' His glance on her face was puzzled.

'Oh yes, I'd forgotten.' She would have to go now. She could not stay here trying to make conversation, not with David watching her all the time with that far too perceptive stare.

'Is anything wrong, Carla?' he asked now. 'You seem to be — not quite yourself.'

'No, everything's fine,' she insisted as she turned to make her exit. 'Goodnight, and sleep well.'

Robin was getting impatient, she discovered. 'I thought you were never coming — ' he complained. 'Why not come back to my place now? At least you'll be off duty there, and we can take up where we left off the other night. It could be fun — '

Carla shook her head. 'Not tonight, Robin. I'm tired — '

'You'll be fine, once you get away from here. This place inhibits you, just as it used to do Giselle. It makes you think old, when you should be thinking young. You don't belong here, you belong with me. I can make you forget all about this place, I was beginning to make you forget the other night, wasn't I?'

She could not answer because of the pressure of his mouth on her own, the strength of his body against hers, as she fought to free herself from a caress that was too intimate by far.

'No, Robin, you are wrong about me — ' she protested.

He laughed. 'I don't think so. I think you are a

tease, Carla — '

Panic filled Carla, then into the panic came a voice from behind her, a voice cold with fury. David's voice. 'And I think it's time you left. Or do you want to be thrown out?'

Robin shrugged as he released Carla. 'No, I'll go willingly. I can see your point, Doctor. It would be bad luck if you were to lose your little cook, wouldn't it? Or is she more to you than just your little cook? If so, it could make things rather awkward for you, for both of you. Couldn't it?'

As he spoke, Robin directed a mocking glance at David Ross. Then with a nod of amusement at Carla he called out a cheerful 'Goodnight, darling,' and made his way coolly out of the kitchen, and out of the house.

When he had gone, Carla and David still stood there listening to the sound of his car engine growing fainter and fainter.

'I'm sorry,' Carla whispered when it had finally died away. 'So sorry, David.'

Eight

'I'm sorry too,' David said in a low voice.

'But it wasn't your fault,' she interrupted. 'It was mine, for going out with Robin in the first place. For allowing him to imagine — ' She could not go on.

'To imagine that you were attracted to him?' he finished for her.

Carla sighed. 'Yes. I suppose I. was flattered because he begged me to go out with him at a time when I was feeling very low and rejected. I know you tried to warn me, David. You must think me very stupid, that I asked for trouble and got what I deserved.' She raised her eyes to his, pleading for his understanding, his forgiveness.

He smiled sadly at her. 'We rarely get what we deserve, Carla. We do what we think is best, at the time, but it can still go wrong. There's no need to apologise for that.'

'There's need to apologise for what he said to you. I've never given him any reason to think — to believe — that I was anything more to you, that I am anything more to you than your — ' Now that she had gone so far she found that she could not go on and say the rest. There was a great lump swelling inside her throat, a great emotion filling her mind.

David was looking at her thoughtfully. 'I don't suppose you have, Carla. Morag must have told him she saw us together at the teashop that day. Though God knows, it was an innocent enough outing.'

'I never saw Morag.'

'She arrived just as I was buying the chocolates. You were looking in the shop window, but I saw her give you a long look as though she might come to speak to you, then she seemed to change her mind.'

It would have to be Morag who had seen them. Morag, who had shown her disappointment because David was not present when she came to the manor with her brother, Morag, who had said more than once that she would like to help David solve his problems. Well she had done nothing but create another worry for him now, Carla knew, if she had put the idea into her brother's mind that David was too fond of Carla.

'I didn't think Robin would turn so nasty,' she said slowly.

'You didn't realise he would be so jealous, did you?'

Carla stared at him, uncomprehending. 'But he had nothing to be jealous of. I mean, it's not as if — ' She broke off as colour flooded her face.

'Were you going to say that it's not as if you *were* more to me than just my little cook?' he asked quietly.

She nodded, aware suddenly of where they were heading and wanting to stop the course of events, but knowing that she was unable to do so because David was lifting her chin with one finger and searching her face with his half-tender, half-sad eyes.

'But you are so much more to me than that, though I didn't realise it until this evening when I saw him with his hands on you.'

'Oh, David,' she whispered.

'I thought, until then, that I just liked you and admired the way you had tackled a difficult job that you were not used to doing, the patience you had with Bessie and the other old dears. I had not admitted to myself how much I longed to get back here every day just to see you, even if I hardly had time to talk to you,' he added with a rueful grin. 'Perhaps I ought not to have told you. It isn't fair to you because I'm eleven years older than you and I've far too many responsibilities, and far too many problems. Nothing to offer you, except my love.'

'It's too late to tell me that. Too late to warn me off, David.' As she said the words she slipped her arms about his neck and lifted her mouth for his kiss. They clung to each other then as though they would never let go, but the flame of joy that illuminated the first long embraces was soon tempered by the remembrance of the problems David had mentioned.

'I can offer you nothing right now but this,' he warned. 'Even if I were free, which I am not yet, I'm only a country doctor with too little spare time, and all my mother's responsibilities on my shoulders as well as my own just now. It's a time when everything has been going wrong for me, except for meeting you.'

'Perhaps you need me to make it all come right again?' she said softly.

'Oh yes, I need you, Carla my love, but is it fair for me to ask you to wait for me until I'm free?'

'That's for me to decide, isn't it, David?'

He kissed her mouth, her eyes, her hair, then drew her down on to the shabby sofa which stood in the bay window of the kitchen and began to tell her about his failed marriage.

'I met Giselle when I went to work at an American hospital for a year before coming into the practice here, and married her too quickly. Later, when the year was almost over, she began to put pressure on me to stay in America, but I knew it was not for me. Besides, my father was dying and I wanted to be here to do what I could for him and Mother. I thought when Giselle saw how good life could be here she would settle down in the house my parents had given us for a wedding present and be happy with friends, a family, a dog. She was never happy here, though, not even in the beginning. She said it was too quiet and she didn't like living in the country, that she missed her American friends and city life. It was not long before she began to look for distractions, and then the gossip began.' Pain shadowed his eyes as he remembered.

'How awful for you.'

'I didn't believe the gossip at first, until the night I was unwell and had to leave the Health Centre during surgery time. I went home to the Ford House and they were there together. It was not the first time they'd been there together while

I was working. Giselle seemed to be quite relieved that it was all in the open at last. She said we'd get a divorce because she knew she could never enjoy being a country doctor's wife. We arranged that she would go back to America and have time to think it over first, but I think I knew that she would not come back to me. That it was just a matter of waiting for the divorce to go through.'

'So you are divorced?' Carla could not keep the hopeful note out of her voice.

'I ought to have been, but there was a complication because Giselle was ill soon after returning to America. It seems to have held things up. That did not worry me at first, since there was no-one else in my life. I just let things drift. Now I wish I hadn't.'

'Where does Robin fit into the picture? He is involved, isn't he?' Carla asked with a frown.

David shrugged his sturdy shoulders. 'I don't know that he comes into it at all now. I think Giselle was just someone to share a brief relationship with, as he was to her. I was so angry and upset that I just told her to go, and not to come back if she could not be trusted. I suppose I stopped loving her then. Later, when she was ready to go and I'd had time to cool off a bit, I said we would see how we both felt when we'd been apart for a while. I think I knew she wouldn't come back, and that if she did I would not be able to trust her. There has to be trust between people, especially when one of them is a country doctor. You have to be very careful about gossip in a place like Ravensford, Carla.'

Those last few words hung in the air between

them, so that restraint fell upon them. There was a warning sound about them, to Carla's ears, because hadn't Morag Muir already linked her name with that of David simply because she had seen them leaving a teashop in a town a few miles away together? Was David trying to spell out to her how careful they must be that gossip did not link *their* names?

'It won't be easy for us, will it, David?' Her eyes were troubled as they met his.

'No, because every look I give you, every word I say to you must betray how I feel about you.'

'So it would be better if I kept away from you as much as possible? Is that what you want me to do, David?' she asked sadly.

'Oh, God, no! It's not what I want! I want to show all the world that I love you. I want to shout it from the fells, and across the river. I want to take you into my home and into my life the way I've already taken you into my heart, Carla. But to do that before I am free will harm us both, and maybe the practice I share with my partners.'

'Will it be better for you if I go away, David? Move on to some other job right away from here?'

'It might be better for *you*, Carla. As for myself, I don't know how I'd cope without you, now. You've given hope and joy to my days, don't take it away from me, will you?'

He pulled her to her feet as the old wall clock above their heads struck the hour of one and held her fast against him so that she could feel the strain as well as the longing that was in him. A longing that was matched by her own. 'Stay, if you can, my love,' he begged. 'I'll try not to make it too difficult for you. Or for myself,' he ended with a sigh.

'I'll stay,' she promised. 'For as long as you need me.'

'I'll always need you. Oh God, I wish I didn't need you so much, then I might be able to think only of you and send you away.'

'I'll never want to leave you,' she murmured against his lips. 'Never.'

Yet he sent her away soon afterwards, subduing his own hunger for her in the knowledge that it would be so easy to persuade her, and himself, that it was right for him to make love to her in this silent house of sleeping people. But Carla might be regretful in the morning, and then he would lose her.

So, 'Go to bed, my love,' he ordered. 'Before I forget all my good resolutions.'

For a long moment she stared into his face, waiting for him to weaken as she longed for him to do. Then he shook his head and put her gently away from him. 'Sleep well, my dearest,' he said.

How could she sleep well when her whole being ached for him, when every part of her longed to be with him? If he had not sent her away . . .

Yet she knew that David had sent her away to save her perhaps from future pain and regret. Because he was afraid that once she had allowed her feelings to run away with her there would be no turning back. Being honest with herself, she knew that it would have been so. His care and concern for her brought a small glow of comfort to her before she at last drifted into sleep.

When she woke early the next morning her

Doctor David

thoughts were immediately going back to the night before, wondering if it really could be true that David loved her so much, wanted her so much. If he did, she would wait for him for however long it took him to get his freedom, but she must be so careful not to betray her feelings for him in front of other people in case there was harmful gossip. David had suffered enough at the hands of the gossips, he should not suffer again because of her, she vowed.

Another problem came into her mind once she was downstairs in the kitchen and had greeted David with the sort of casual 'good morning' that she would have given on any other day. As he ate his breakfast she turned her thoughts to the planning of meals, and shopping for them. Shopping would mean going to the Muirs' market garden, and it would not be easy to meet Robin calmly again after the way he had treated her last night.

'Would it upset your mother if I stopped buying things from the Muirs?' she asked hesitantly when she took more toast in for David. 'It's going to be awkward for me, isn't it?'

'Yes,' he replied, frowning. 'Because Mother has a soft spot for Robin, and a thing about only buying really fresh vegetables for her old dears. The Muirs are the only local growers, you see. You would have to go much further afield to buy what you need, but of course if you can't face Robin that's what you must do. We'll have to think of some excuse to give Mother then when she comes home.'

'I don't want to upset her by making changes while she is away,' Carla said quickly. 'I don't want there to be any gossip about why we are not friendly with the Muirs any more, either,' she added. 'I can manage without going down there today, and I might be feeling braver about facing Robin tomorrow.'

David smiled as he put up a hand to touch her cheek lightly. 'After what I said to him last night he might have got the message now that you are not very interested in him.'

Carla had her doubts about that, though she did not voice them to David. So she was more than surprised by the correctness of Robin's behaviour when next she visited the Muirs' market garden. There was no indication in his manner as he greeted her that she was anything more to him than just another regular customer, in fact she was impressed by his respectful attitude, his charm and his courtesy. It was easy to understand why Mrs Ross liked him, and why Bessie and some of the other elderly ladies from the manor adored him. It was not until she had chosen all the produce she required and Robin had carried it out to her car that he referred to the events which lingered still so close to the surface of her mind.

'No hard feelings about the other night, Carla, I hope?'

She hesitated for a long moment, then shook her head.

'Sorry if I upset you. I just got a bit carried away, and I was under the impression that you felt the same about me.'

'I've never given you any reason to think that,' she protested.

'You didn't seem to object on the night we went

back to my place from the Miller's Inn,' he reminded her with a challenging glance.

'That was before I — ' She broke off, shocked at how close she had come to giving herself away.

'Before you what, Carla?'

She recovered herself quickly and managed a laugh. 'Before I learned that you wouldn't take "no" for an answer.'

That brought a grin from him. 'Perhaps I did push it a bit, but you tempted me, Carla, glowing there like a newly-opened flower in that house full of fading blooms. It was a pity your cold fish of a doctor had to come in just then.'

'He's not a cold fish,' she said unwisely.

'That's not what his wife thought, but maybe you know him better than she did, Carla?'

'He's my boss's son, that's all, to me,' she lied.

'Well, just keep it that way, for your own sake my dear. Otherwise it could be awkward for you if the lovely Giselle decides to come back.'

'But she won't, will she — ' Carla began, then knew that the words would have been better left unsaid.

Robin was looking at her through narrowed eyes. 'Is that what he told you?'

'We haven't discussed it,' she lied again.

'It isn't what she says in her letters to me. I think she's keeping her options open. That could be worth remembering, Carla.'

'It's of no interest to me whether she comes back or not. I don't know what gave you the idea that it might be. All I'm interested in is getting the next meal on the table at the manor, and if I don't hurry I'll be late in doing that.'

Carla did not stop to see if she had convinced Robin. All she wanted was to be away from him, and away from his hateful reminder that David was still married to Giselle, even if he loved *her*. Yet Robin's words remained to haunt her, day and night, so that soon she was not sleeping well.

Ought she perhaps to move on, in case Giselle Ross *did* come back? she asked herself sometimes. Yet she had promised David that she would stay and help him through this crisis and keep his extended family together until his mother was well enough to take over again. It was hard for her to subdue her love for him and her longing for him when she had to face him so often, speak to him so often. Even to be alone with him sometimes when the old people had all gone to bed and the manor was silent.

These were the hardest times of all, the times when a shared look across an empty room induced in her an almost unbearable desire to run into his arms. When she could guess from the set of his jaw and the taut line of his mouth that he was struggling against the same temptation as she was, the need to love each other fully and without restraint.

There was a night when all his firm resolutions, all her own self-discipline, were put to the test. It began with the news that David's mother would be returning to her home that weekend, quite fit again and ready to take charge of the manor. This news brought such excitement to her paying guests, so many plans for her welcome home. Plans for a special meal, with the old gentlemen gathering money together to buy bottles of champagne, while the ladies would purchase flowers for her.

After so much discussion, and quite a few differences of opinion between some of the residents, they were all tired and ready to go to bed early, Carla, too, was tired and exhausted from answering so many questions about the celebration meal she was going to provide. There had been differences of opinion about that as well, since so many of Mrs Ross's friends had assumed that they knew what she would like best. Now the discussions were over and everyone had gone to bed, all except for Carla and David who were alone in the firelit lounge. Both knew that they should say 'goodnight', neither of them could bring themselves to do so because from now on there would be less chance of spending time alone together.

'We won't be alone like this tomorrow evening, Carla. We'll have to meet somewhere else, if we can,' David said.

Carla felt her throat swell. 'We'll have to be so careful, won't we? Not to cause gossip, and not to let your mother guess how we feel about one another.'

He sighed. 'That'll be that hardest part. Once she gets to know you and sees us together, it won't be long before she knows. If only I were free, Carla. I hate all the uncertainty, hate being in the same house as you and having to stay away from you. That's why I'm thinking of going back to live in the Ford House, once Mother is home.'

'Are you, David? Wouldn't it be better if I went away instead? You could get Mrs Golightly's younger daughter to come and do the cooking, now that her job at the hotel is finished.' It hurt to make that suggestion when she could not endure the thought of days, weeks perhaps, when she would not see David, yet she felt compelled to do so by the picture in her mind of David returning at the end of his long work filled days to an empty and comfortless home where no one waited up to make him a hot drink or even just to listen to him talking about his worries.

'Don't go, Carla. Please don't go! I can't face life without you, now.'

In a few swift strides he crossed the room and pulled her into his arms to hold her so close that she could feel his heart hammering against her own. Desperately, they clung together, their bodies aching with need, with love long denied. Both were aware that there was no one to know whether they surrendered at last to their overwhelming passion for one another.

'I love you so much,' he said as he sank with her on to the low chintz-covered sofa. 'Too much to go on waiting.'

'I love you the same, darling David,' Carla whispered.

Outside the house the storm that had been raging for most of the day grew worse, with gale force winds hurling hailstones at the windows, but Carla and David were unaware of it, unaware of everything except themselves and their love.

It was Bessie's voice, breaking into the darkened room, that shattered their joy.

'Are you deaf, Doctor David?' she demanded. 'Didn't you hear the phone? They want you out with the unit to an accident.'

'Right, Bessie. Go back to bed. Sorry I didn't

hear,' Carla heard him say. She stayed there while he stumbled away towards the thin stream of light which shone through the partly open door into the hall. A moment later she heard his voice asking the police officer on the other end of the line for the location of the accident. Then there was the slam of the back door, a powerful engine roaring into life. Before she had managed to pull herself together sufficiently to leave the sofa the Immediate Care Unit was on its way at speed down the drive; a mobile surgery which could mean life or death for those involved in a serious accident.

David did not belong to her now, Carla knew. He belonged to those people, as he would always belong to those who needed him. She could only wait for him, and pray for them.

Nine

Carla gazed out of the window into the storm-tossed night, but she was too late to catch a glimpse of the sturdy vehicle which housed the mobile surgery known as the Immediate Care Unit. She had seen this parked outside Ravensford Manor at times when David was on call with the unit, but this was the first time she had been there when it was called out. As she turned away from the window she became aware that Figaro was filling the air with his desolation. Eerie howls echoed from the conservatory. Figaro was used to being left behind, so it was probably the storm which had upset him, she decided. She made her way to him, anxious to quieten him before he roused all the elderly residents.

'Poor old boy,' she whispered to him. 'We'll keep each other company till your master comes back.'

She took him with her into the lounge, where she re-kindled the fire, and he promptly fell asleep on the hearthrug while she tried to imagine what David was doing at that moment. The pictures her vivid imagination conjured up made her afraid for David. There would be trees coming down on such a night, and the driving rain would make visibility difficult. She knew, from what David had told her, that the unit was often used when victims were trapped in their vehicles as firemen worked to free them, so there must also be the danger of fire or explosion from igniting petrol or from some of the dangerous fluids carried by tankers. It was hazardous work, even if you were used to it.

For what seemed like many hours she sat there listening for the first indication that David was safe, but the only sounds she heard were those of the big dog snoring at her feet and the furious wind tearing at the walls of the old house. She was too uneasy even to doze off. All she could do was sit there and think of all that had happened since she came to Ravensford Manor, how she had come here feeling lonely and rejected, jealous of her sister for stealing Emile. Yet in the weeks since then she had learned to forget her loneliness and jealousy as she got more and more deeply involved with Mrs Ross's unusual paying guests. Now they did not seem at all odd to her, Bessie the dwarf, Paolo, the flamboyant ex-magician, Toby Wren the retired trapeze artiste and Jacob the former strong man from a circus, because now they were her friends. Just as David was her dearest of friends, as well as her beloved.

One day she would have the right to wait for David's homecoming as his wife, down at the Ford House. He had told her tonight that this was his dearest wish. In the meantime, she would have a kettle boiling ready to make him a hot drink when he came home, and she would make sandwiches too, since it was many hours since he had eaten.

The clock high up on the kitchen wall showed almost two o'clock. David had been gone for over two hours now. Because she found the emptiness of the kitchen oppressive, she switched on the radio for company and caught the ending of a pop record. Then it was time for the hourly news bulletin, and the news tonight was mostly connected with the severe weather. It brought flood warnings for some areas and warnings of expected structural damage for others, as well as news of a spate of weather related accidents. Carla's hands grew still in the act of making ham sandwiches.

'A serious accident is reported from the market town of Ravensbridge, where a large tree has fallen on to the cab of a petrol tanker trapping the driver and his mate. Firemen and police are working to cut them free of the wreckage.'

So that was where David would be at this minute with his mobile surgery. Of course the rescue bid could be all over now, she tried to comfort herself as the howling of the wind increased in volume. Soon she would hear the Immediate Care Unit approaching the house, and her anxiety would be over, for the time being. The thought slipped away from her as the front door bell began to ring loudly and insistently as though being pushed by impatient fingers. If it did not stop the old dears would be awakened and filled with alarm, especially now that Figaro was adding his deep bark.

She raced along the hall, and reached the front door at the same time as the dog, who was now growling ferociously. With one hand she restrained him, while undoing the bolt with the

other. It could not be burglars, she reasoned. They
would not be likely to ring for admittance, would
they? It was too late to have such thoughts, anyway, with the door half open and a figure being
hurled inwards by the wind.

Carla's eyes widened as she took her first clear
glance at the female form, the long, streaming wet
hair, the muddied clothes, the ashen face. No
words of explanation came from the woman at
first, just a series of shuddering sighs that were
quite unnerving.

'What do you want?' she heard herself ask. 'Are
you hurt? Do you need help?'

No answers came, but the shivering and shuddering sighs went on. The skin of the woman's
face was grey looking, the eyes half-closed.

'Are you ill? Is it the doctor you want to see?'
Carla asked urgently as Figaro advanced cautious-
ly and tried to lick one of the slack hands. The
woman shied away from him.

'Lie down, Figaro!' Carla ordered. Then, since
the woman was so obviously very ill, she added,
'I'll ring for an ambulance. The doctor isn't here
just now. He's had to go to an accident.'

As she finished speaking a peal of laughter,
weird and mirthless, issued from the woman's
mouth. It sent a shiver of apprehension down
Carla's spine. Was the woman an escapee from a
mental hospital? Then, as the figure got to its feet
and began to stagger across the hall, a new suspicion came to her. The figure swayed and collapsed
into one of the big carver chairs, knocking over a
tall vase of chrysanthemums so that flowers and
water cascaded over her already sodden clothing.

'So the doctor's out? I should have known he would be. The doctor's always out. Always doing his job. No time for anything else. Always the perfect bloody family doctor. The perfect English doctor, Doctor David Ross!'

The sentence finished with another outburst of hysterical laughter. Was the woman one of David's patients, Carla wondered then. Whoever she was, Carla knew that she must quieten her before she disturbed the whole household. If she could just get her away into the back of the house it might help, because here the noise she was making was rising and filling the hall and staircase.

'Would you like some hot coffee, or tea? I've already got a kettle on the boil,' she said desperately.

This brought another burst of wild laughter. 'Need more than tea or coffee. Want some of Doctor David's brandy.'

'I can't give you that.'

'No need. I can get it for myself.'

On her feet again, the woman was making for the door of David's office. She would have to stop her, Carla knew, but how? With a great surge of relief she heard Bessie come clumping down the stairs, grumbling about the noise.

'It's like Piccadilly Circus here tonight,' the dwarf began. She stopped on the third step from the bottom. 'Mrs Ross!' she exclaimed. 'Whatever are you doing here? You're supposed to be in America.'

The woman stopped with one hand on the office door, holding herself up with an effort as she tried to focus her glazed eyes on Bessie's hostile face.

Then she let out another burst of mirthless laughter.

'I've come to see my husband, of course.'

Carla felt as if all the breath had been knocked out of her body. David's wife, this pathetic creature! All these weeks she had been imagining someone young and very beautiful, glamorous and exciting enough to be easily able to find other men for company while David was working. Never had she dreamed that she would feel pity for David's wife. On the heels of that thought came another, why had Giselle come here tonight? Why did she want to see David?

It was Figaro who gave warning in that moment that David was back. He gave a series of ecstatic barks as he raced to the back door the moment he heard the Immediate Care Unit come to a halt there. David bent to stroke his head as he entered the house, then stood for a moment, immobile, listening to the commotion that could be heard coming from the hall. A few swift paces brought him face to face with the hysterical woman, while Carla watched, sick to the depths of her being.

'Giselle.' He said it so quietly, so calmly, as though the unexpected appearance of his estranged wife were not the last straw for him on this traumatic night. 'What are you doing here?'

'I came to see you,' she responded mockingly.

'Why, when you haven't even bothered to answer my letters for some time?'

'I came because I need money. There's no other reason why I'd come.'

'But I sent you money. I've been sending it regularly — '

'Not enough though, Doctor. Not enough to buy the stuff I need. The stuff I can't do without. I need some right now. I was just going to get it — '

She took a lurching step forward as she said that and Carla saw David move quickly to put his hands on her shoulders to steady her.

'I'd say you'd had enough of that stuff already,' he told her sternly. Then, as his fingers made contact with her soaking wet clothes, he asked, 'How did you get so wet? Where have you come from?'

'From the ford. I'm not so fond of you that I'd get wet through walking to see you, but I got the car stuck in the ford and had to leave it there,' the slurred voice told him.

'You shouldn't have been driving at all in that state. You sure you just got the car stuck? You haven't been in an accident?'

'No, at least, I don't think so. There was only me. I was going to see Robin, but I didn't get that far, so I came here instead.'

David closed his eyes momentarily as though he could no longer bear to look at her. Then, without looking at Carla, he said, 'Go and make some strong coffee, please, Carla.'

Carla hurried away, and as she did so heard him order Bessie to go back to bed. When she returned with the coffee she found that he had carried Giselle into the lounge and laid her on one of the sofas there. He was just completing the taking of her pulse, and his face was grave. As she set down the tray he did not speak to her but went at once to the telephone to call for an ambulance. She listened to his voice with her heart beating fast.

'I can't bring her in myself because I'm on call with the ICU. I've just got back from an accident, and there could be more before the night is over,' he was explaining to someone at the cottage hospital.

'Bring a blanket, please Carla,' he said when he came back into the lounge. Already he was stripping the wet clothing from his wife's unresisting body and dropping it in a pile at his feet.

'I want brandy,' Giselle was saying when Carla came back with the blanket and one of her own nightgowns. 'Get me some brandy.'

'You've had enough. Too much, in fact,' David told her. 'You are going to hospital as soon as the ambulance gets here. They'll be able to look after you better than we can.'

'Your precious mother won't want to look after me, will she? She doesn't like me, does she, David?'

'Mother isn't here. She's been ill and she's away convalescing,' he told her.

'I want some brandy, then I'll go. I'll go to the Ford House. I'm not going to hospital. I've seen enough of hospitals,' Giselle insisted.

Carla's heart sank. Poor David, having to cope with this on top of the bad road accident he had just attended.

'I can't take you to the Ford House, Giselle. There's no heating on there, and no beds made up. You couldn't possibly stay there on your own. Be sensible for once, for your own sake, please. Let the hospital help you, while there's still time.'

Quite suddenly then Giselle's face crumpled, the animosity faded from it and was replaced by sadness.

'It's too late for me to be sensible, isn't it, David?' she whispered.

Carla felt her own throat constrict as David answered his wife gently, his eyes full of compassion.

'It's never too late, Giselle. Just give us the chance to help you, that's all I ask.'

There was silence for a while, except for the scream of the wind as it hit the solid stone walls of the old house, then Giselle spoke in a voice so low that Carla could only just hear.

'I guess I haven't been very good to you, David, have I? I've brought you a lot of worry − '

'Hush, my dear, don't talk about it now,' he begged.

'Hold my hand, David, please. I'm frightened, so frightened − '

'There's nothing to be afraid of at the cottage hospital, Giselle. They'll look after you, and I'll be in to see you tomorrow.'

Carla watched as he put an arm protectively about the frail figure, supporting her head on his shoulder. She crept out of the room then, unable to bear any more. With legs that felt like lead she climbed the stairs until she came to her room. All at once she felt utterly exhausted, her mind and body numbed by the events of the night. She kicked off her shoes and wriggled out of her skirt, then slid beneath the duvet too tired to remove any of her other clothes.

Yet once in bed she was tormented by the sound of the gale battering her window, and by the picture of David sitting with his arms about his wife telling her that everything was going to be all right. Just as if she still meant all the world to him. Giselle had looked like a child in that moment, a lovely frail child who needed David to cherish and care for her. Carla had seen the caring in his eyes, the look of sad resignation about his mouth, and knew that he would be torn now between his love for her and his loyalty to the sick woman who was still his wife.

Perhaps loyalty would win, she had to face that. Perhaps as he helped Giselle to recover all his old feeling for her would return. There would be no room for her then. Nothing left for her but suffering and loss on a scale she had never before encountered.

It would be better if she left before that happened, Carla decided in that bleak moment. As soon as David's mother was settled in again and able to look after things at Ravensford Manor she would tell her that she was going back to the bookshop for her sister's wedding and would not return. She could make the excuse that her father would need her after her sister had left. So much easier for her if she put David out of her life completely rather than torturing herself with the sight of him being reunited with Giselle.

As the wind abated slightly she heard the ambulance hurtle up the drive and come to a halt. Voices sounded far below, then the slam of doors before the vehicle roared away. Carla turned her face into the pillow and wept.

Ten

'Wake up! Wake up, Carla!'

Bessie's none too gentle hands shook Carla into a state of awareness at last, when she seemed to have only just fallen asleep. She opened her eyes and stared with disbelief at her bedside clock, which told her she ought to have been downstairs three quarters of an hour ago.

'Oh, Bessie, I'm sorry,' she gasped as she swung her legs to the floor. As she did so a wave of faintness enveloped her. Lack of sleep, she told herself as she splashed cold water on her face before pulling on the skirt she had discarded last night. She looked down with distaste at the crumpled blouse in which she had slept, then dragged it off and took the first cotton top she came to in her top drawer to replace it. Only time then to pull a brush through her hair a couple of times before she ran down to join Bessie in the kitchen.

Bessie was plainly in a foul mood, and there was no sign of David, who ought by now to have been eating his breakfast. Why had not Bessie made a start on preparing it, Carla wondered crossly, then put the thought into words.

'Couldn't you have made a start on the doctor's

145

breakfast, Bessie? Or come and woken me sooner?'

'No need,' Bessie retorted tartly. 'Doctor didn't want any breakfast. He's already gone.'

'Oh, was he called out?'

'Not that I know of. He might have gone to the hospital to see *her*.'

'Do you know if he's walked Figaro yet?'

'He said would you do it.'

Carla sighed. There was a dragging ache at the base of her spine and the last thing she felt like was tugging at the end of Figaro's lead on this storm-tossed morning. 'I'll take him after breakfast. It's going to be one of those days, isn't it? And I did want everything going smoothly for when Mrs Ross gets back.'

Bessie did not reply. She was upset about something this morning. Was it just because she had slept in, Carla wondered, or was it to do with the fact that in the moment she had opened the lounge door last night to tell David that he was needed on the telephone she had caught a glimpse of him embracing Carla in the darkened room? It was not easy to tell, and Carla could not ask her, so it was a relief to her when the rest of the inhabitants of the manor began to drift downstairs and she could begin to serve their breakfasts.

There was much talk between them of the storm and the havoc it had caused throughout the North, according to the news bulletins on radio and television. Also speculation about whether Mrs Ross would be delayed by this, but no gossip as yet about the homecoming of the younger Mrs Ross. That would come later, Carla guessed.

As soon as she could after the arrival of Mrs

Golightly and the daughter who helped in the house two or three times a week, Carla told Bessie that she was going to walk Figaro.

'What about your breakfast? You can't go out in this weather with no hot food inside you,' Bessie said, looking at her drawn face with concern.

'I can't eat anything, Bessie. My throat hurts and I've got such a headache. I'll probably feel better when I've had some fresh air.'

'I'm not surprised you've a headache. Up nearly all night, and all that upset! Why did *she* have to come back now? Why couldn't she stay away? She'll only cause trouble, like she did before — '

'Hush, Bessie! The others will hear you,' Carla warned. The elderly people loved a bit of local scandal, she had discovered.

'They'll have to know, sooner or later. Mrs Ross'll be very put out when she hears, I can tell you.'

At least Bessie did not seem to be upset with *her*, Carla thought with a surge of relief as she left the house with Figaro, and that was important on this day when there was so much extra to do before Mrs Ross arrived. Soon the tugging of the big dog at the end of his lead was more than she could put up with, so she let him have his freedom and was not surprised when he made for the Ford House. As she followed at a slower pace she saw David's car parked at the gate. Figaro was already circling it excitedly, having taken a short cut through the ford.

Since she would have to get him back, Carla also approached the ford. Even before she reached the hump-backed bridge she was able to see the vehicle which David's wife had been forced to abandon the night before at the height of the storm. The driver's door was wide open to reveal a flooded interior. No wonder Giselle had been in such a state, after having to wade through several feet of floodwater before making her way up the steep hill to the manor. If she had collapsed on the way and lain undiscovered for many hours, she might not have survived in her weakened state. Carla pushed that thought away from her with an effort as David came to meet her on the bridge.

'Carla,' he said softly as their eyes met and held. His were desolate pools in his haggard face. Her own filled with tears which she brushed away impatiently.

'David,' she whispered, pressing her hands hard on the stonework of the bridge to prevent herself from reaching out for him. She would not do that ever again, now that his wife was back.

His hands came to rest on top of hers, so that she could not turn to escape from him as she might have done.

'I'm so sorry about last night,' he began awkwardly.

'There's no need to apologise,' she broke in hurriedly. 'You were lonely, and I was too vulnerable. It was as much my fault — '

'Stop it Carla!' he said roughly. 'Don't deliberately misunderstand me. I'm not apologising for what happened between us. I'm trying to say I'm sorry for what you had to put up with from Giselle.'

She took a deep breath while the ground beneath her feet shifted then steadied again. 'It wasn't your fault. How — how is she this morning?'

'Critically ill. I don't know how she managed to get out of the car and up the hill to the house in her condition. I came to get some things for her from the Ford House, since all her luggage is wet through.'

'She must have wanted to see you very much — '

His mouth twisted. 'You heard what she said — '

'Maybe she didn't know what she was saying — ' A fit of shivering seized Carla as she finished speaking. 'I must go, there's a lot to do today before your mother comes home.'

'You are cold too, you don't look — '

'Yes, I am cold,' she agreed. 'I expect I'll be warm by the time I get back, at Figaro's speed.'

'Here, Figaro!' David called to the dog who had given chase to a rabbit. 'Go home with Carla.'

It was those few simple words that brought into her mind all that she would lose when she left Ravensford. All that had come to mean so much to her, the man and the dog, the place and the people. All had become precious to her during her time there. Her throat ached with unshed tears as she stumbled away without a backward glance at David.

Back at the manor, a more subdued atmosphere had taken over as news of Giselle Ross's return had spread among the residents, but there was still much delight because their beloved hostess was on her way home. By early afternoon the storm was over and pale sunshine was shining on the furniture which Mrs Golightly and her daughter had polished to perfection. When the flowers Carla

was to collect from the market garden were added
the air of welcome would be complete, but Carla
was dreading her trip to the market garden. Then
she had an idea, which she voiced while serving
coffee to Miss Clare and Mavis.

'As you are buying the flowers, ladies, for Mrs
Ross would you like to come with me to the market
garden to choose them?'

'What a splendid idea!' Miss Clare responded
graciously. 'We'd love to do that, wouldn't we,
Mavis?'

Mavis agreed enthusiastically, and Carla felt an
enormous sense of relief because she would not
have to face Robin Muir alone now that he must
almost certainly have heard that Giselle Ross was
back. When they arrived at the market garden
Robin and Morag both came to greet them cheerfully, though Carla felt very conscious of them
both eyeing her speculatively. Then the moment
she had been dreading was upon her.

'We must find our very best blooms for this
special day, carnations and spray chrysanthemums I think.' Then Robin turned his smile on
Carla. 'A special day indeed, since young Mrs Ross
has also come home. Don't you agree, Carla?'

'Yes, of course.'

She began to make her own choice of fruit and
vegetables hurriedly while Morag took the two old
ladies to choose flowers in one of the glasshouses.
When they had done that, they decided that they
would like a pot plant as well.

'Morag will show you what we have while I pack
the flowers,' Robin told them.

When they had disappeared into yet another

greenhouse he turned a mocking look on Carla. 'Were you afraid to face me on your own? Is that why you needed to bring them?' he asked.

'I don't know what you mean — '

'Afraid I'd say "I told you so"?' he persisted.

That stung Carla. 'Wasn't it partly your fault that she went away in the first place? That the marriage broke up?'

He laughed shortly. 'Is that what he told you? It was *his* fault, Carla, that she left. He was too involved with his work for a woman like Giselle. She was bored and she didn't fit in with his way of life. Didn't even try to fit in. So she was always on the lookout for men who weren't too tied up with their work. I was just one of them. I could tell you others, but I won't. Giselle is a lovely woman but I like my girls quieter, steadier. In fact, Carla, I think I must be ready for marriage. At least, my thoughts have been turning more and more to that since you came here.'

'Don't include me in your plans,' she told him. 'I'll be leaving here soon to go back and work in the family bookshop.'

She ought to feel better now that she had made her decision public, Carla thought, but she didn't. All she could feel was a great sense of loss, of a build up of misery inside her that she tried hard to hide from Miss Clare and her friend as they drove back to the manor. It was only a short journey but all the time she was conscious of the pain and sorrow that enveloped her, real physical pain with a thumping headache which made concentration difficult, and sorrow because she kept remembering Robin's final words to her.

'You are making a mistake in running away,' he had said, but she had brushed his words away angrily just as she was now trying to banish them to the back of her mind.

She was touched when, as she handed the pot plant to little Mavis on their arrival at the manor, Mavis handed it back to her with the words, 'We wanted you to have this, my dear, for your own room because you've been so kind to us all and looked after us all so well while Mrs Ross has been ill.'

Carla felt her throat swell as she bent to kiss Mavis, and then Miss Clare. She felt the same emotion when Paolo Peacock presented her with the box of liqueur chocolates which had been ordered along with the champagne.

'A token of esteem from us old pros', my dear young lady,' he told her gallantly.

How she would miss these delightful old-timers when she was back in London, Carla mused as she carried the chocolates and the plant to her room. While she was there she took a large dose of aspirin in an effort to get rid of the headache that would not seem to go away. It was not just her head that hurt, she realised then, it was her back and her legs and even her hands.

It took a great effort from her to complete the preparations for Mrs Ross's welcome home, and even to go forward with outstretched hand and words of welcome when Mrs Ross stepped out of David's car. She could not meet David's eyes, and was glad to leave him and his mother with the excuse that she had scones to remove from the oven for the afternoon tea.

In the kitchen she was glad of the silence that prevailed because Bessie had joined everyone else in talking excitedly to their hostess and friend. The huge turkey which was to be the main course for the celebration dinner party was already in the oven and the Black Forest gâteau which was to follow rested in the pantry, so all she had to do was concentrate on cooking the vegetables and keep her mind off her aches and pains, she told herself. The cups of tea she swallowed did not ease her burning throat, and soon she was troubled by dizziness, but at last all was ready for the special meal and she was able to relax, though not to eat any of the food she had cooked because her appetite had completely disappeared.

'You had no lunch either,' Bessie scolded. 'What's wrong with you?'

'I'm just tired, I suppose. I'll go to bed early,' Carla told her.

'It's more than that,' she heard Mrs Ross say from a distance. 'You look — '

The rest was lost as darkness descended on her without warning. When she came to, David was taking her pulse. Shortly afterwards she found herself being escorted to her room by Mrs Golightly and Mrs Ross and being put to bed by them.

'I'm so sorry,' she whispered to David's mother, 'for spoiling your party.'

After that she lost all count of time as she succumbed to the virus which had struck so many people in the Ravensford area during the last few weeks. As she drifted in and out of a troubled sleep she was aware that sometimes a doctor, but never David, bent over her and asked her how she felt.

'Why are you here?' she asked him once. Why
you and not David, she meant but perhaps he
misunderstood her because he said only that he
was there to see that she soon recovered from this
nasty type of 'flu. Mrs Golightly, who was looking
after her marvellously, told her that the doctor was
called Abercrombie, and that he had come out of
retirement temporarily to help in the practice.

Why hadn't David been to see her, she longed to
know but could not bring herself to ask Mrs
Golightly. Even Bessie did not come to see her, so
that it seemed to Carla as she gradually began to
feel better that she and Mrs Golightly lived in a
world of their own up here on the top floor of the
house. Yet even Mrs Golightly did not have much
to say to her, though she did tease Carla about the
huge bunch of scented carnations which Robin
Muir had delivered after he heard of her illness.

'You made a conquest there,' she remarked.
'He's a good looking fellow, and he's got a nice
business too.'

'He's only a friend,' Carla told her crossly.

'They all say that,' the older woman replied as
she bustled out of the room again leaving Carla
thoroughly bored and irritated because by now
she was tired of her own company and anxious to
see what was happening downstairs, and especially why David had not come to see her.

'I ought to be getting back to work,' she said
fretfully.

'There's no need for you to worry your head
about that yet. My Jill is in charge of the kitchen
just now, since the hotel where she was working

closed until next season. She has a catering college diploma, you know.'

'Which is more than I've got,' Carla said grumpily.

'You've done a good job since you came here, diploma or not. We all say that, even Bessie,' added Mrs Golightly.

It came to Carla then that if Jill Golightly was now established in the kitchen of Ravensford Manor there was nothing to keep her here, once she was fit enough to travel to London. So she would go as soon as possible. It would be better that way. Less hurtful for her. Less embarrassing for David.

'You can go downstairs this afternoon,' Dr Abercrombie told her that day. 'No going out of doors yet though in this freezing wind.'

'Thank you, Doctor,' Carla said meekly.

'I won't be seeing you again. It's back to my books and my garden for me now that the practice is fully manned again. Don't overdo things at first, will you?'

'I won't,' she promised.

It was so good to walk down the stairs that afternoon even though her legs did feel a bit unsteady. So good to be welcomed by all the old dears, who told her how much they had missed her. To be urged into the chair nearest to the fire in the lounge and be waited on at tea time by Paolo, Jacob and Joe. She felt loved, cherished, and indescribably sad because so soon she would be leaving them all behind. Worst of all, leaving David behind. David, who had been waiting for her at the foot of the stairs, holding out his hand to her while his eyes dwelt on her face. He looked strained and so weary, she thought, as he spoke to her.

'I'm glad to see you, Carla. How are you feeling now?'

'Much better, thank you.' She wanted to ask him how *he* was, and why it had been Dr Abercrombie who had looked after her and not him, but his mother was standing beside him waiting to slip an arm through Carla's and lead her into the lounge.

She did not see David again until it was time for dinner that evening. Nor was there any sign of his wife. Was she still in the cottage hospital, or had she gone away again, Carla wondered. She wanted to ask someone about that but could not bring herself to do so. Neither did anyone volunteer information about Giselle. It was as though she had never come back to Ravensford so unexpectedly on that storm-filled night. Or were they all hiding something from her? This new suspicion stayed with her during the hours between the serving of tea and dinner, until it became a certainty.

It was the black tie David was wearing that confirmed her guess. From the moment she noticed it, when he took his place opposite her at the usual small table, she found it difficult to remain composed as she responded to the small talk maintained by David and his mother. Found it even harder to look at him. All at once, it was impossible. She could not stay there, so close to him, with his mother's eyes resting compassionately first on him then on her. She knows, Carla thought. She has either guessed about us or

David has told her. Mrs Ross was saying something to her now, but Carla did not hear as she got
to her feet so hurriedly that she scattered her table
napkin and silver cutlery as she moved.

'Excuse me, please,' she muttered, not stopping
to pick them up because all she wanted was to
escape.

Somehow she reached the foot of the stairs, but
even her longing to be alone again in her room
was not strong enough to get her beyond the first
few steps before David was beside her, persuad-
ing her gently into his study, closing the door and
lifting her face then so that she was forced to look
at him, really look at *him* and not just at the black
tie.

'You didn't know, did you?' he asked quietly.

She shook her head. 'No. I wanted to ask how
she was, when I saw you this afternoon. Only I
couldn't bring myself to do it, and no one else
mentioned it.'

He sighed. 'Mother asked them not to talk about
it, and they seem to have been very good. I
suppose if Bessie had been about it would have
been more difficult.'

'Mrs Ross says she has the virus now. How ill is
she?'

David laughed. 'Not very. She's been one of the
lucky ones. She'll be down again tomorrow.'

Carla looked down at her hands, trembling
slightly in her lap. 'I'm sorry, David. So sorry,
about Giselle.'

His jaw tightened. 'It was a bad time, but it's
over now. We did everything we could for her, but
it was not enough. She was already desperately ill

when she got here. I knew she couldn't survive for more than a few days. That all I could do was to try and give her comfort at the end. I *had* to do that.'

'I thought, when I saw you with her that night, that there'd be a reconciliation — ' Carla said in a low voice.

'It was too late for that. I had no love left to give her, Carla. All that had finished when she left me. In fact, it finished before then when I knew she was deceiving me. All I had left to give her was my skill as a doctor, and my compassion. I gave her those until the end.'

'Which was — ?'

'Four days ago.'

'How terrible for you, David.' How inadequate the words sounded, when she wanted to say so much more.

'It *was* terrible, at the time, but it's over now. The closing of a chapter that started with such promise and ended with a nightmare. I didn't know myself just what her illness was until I saw her that night. Perhaps I ought to have suspected it, but I didn't.'

'I felt so guilty when I saw her, David.'

'Guilty? Why should you feel guilty about her, Carla?'

'You know why — '

'I'm the one who was guilty. I'm the one who married her and brought her back here to a life she hated. My only excuse is that I was too young and inexperienced to know that it wouldn't work. That she was the wrong wife for someone like me. But I paid for my mistake, Carla. Paid for it with my loneliness and despair. My only consolation was my work, until you came. You showed me how it could have been for me. How it ought to be between a man and his wife. How it will be one day, Carla.'

He lifted her from the deep chair where she had been listening to him and drew her into his arms to kiss her long and tenderly. It was not the time for passion, so his embrace was loving and restrained.

'Do you know what I'm trying to say, even though it's too early yet to say it, my love?'

'Yes, David.'

'Mother says you are going home soon for your sister's wedding,' he went on when she was comfortably settled on his knee. 'But you will come back, won't you? Not here, but to the Ford House.'

'Yes, David,' she said again.

'I shall come down for you,' he decided. 'Then I can meet your father and your sister and your new brother-in-law. We'll have to wait a while, but it will be worth the waiting, when you come back to me. We'll begin a new life together and it'll be a good life.' He smiled down into her pale, relaxed face and added, 'In a few months you'll be a doctor's wife, Carla, but at least you know what you are taking on. You've seen it all in these last weeks, the best and the worst.'

'From now on it'll be the best,' she promised.